QUOTES

QUOTES

Tyrone Harvey

QUOTES

iUniverse books may be ordered through booksellers or by contacting:

iUniverse
1663 Liberty Drive
Bloomington, IN 47403
www.iuniverse.com
844-349-9409

ISBN: 978-1-6632-1623-6 (sc)
ISBN: 978-1-6632-1624-3 (hc)
ISBN: 978-1-6632-1622-9 (e)

Library of Congress Control Number: 2021900486

Print information available on the last page.

iUniverse rev. date: 05/07/2021

This Book is dedicated to
L. O. R. D. and GO GET IT Publishing,
Because each morning I wake up …
I am inspired to GO GET IT.

– FACTS

"LOOK OUT Y'ALL I'M A TIME BOMB TICKIN..."

CHUCK D

Quotes

Blurb

Mysterious things start taking place in Connecticut. Buildings are being blown up, killing people by the hundreds. The news media has spread the word. Believing the Terrorist group known as ZIZI is to blame for committing these foolish acts of terror. The whole state is on edge. No One and no place are safe… Bomb Specialist/F.B.I. Agent Sarah Richardson is assigned to this intense case. When she starts investigating the crime scene, she learns that cruel and unusual punishment is to blame and what begin to unfold is much bigger than ZIZI…. F.B.I agent Sarah Richardson is lead down a dark tunnel where she come face to face with one of the most psychotic individuals ever.

QUOTES

By TYRONE HARVEY

"The quicker you think about it, the faster it's done."

"Your mind becomes a fire pit, ignited by hellish thoughts."

"Good advice comes from being too close to the heat of the fire."

"Making the enemy your friend, will destroy him."

"Victory is the word most heard after war."

"A friend is someone who love you unconditionally, whether right or wrong."

"Death is only a crossing over into paradise."
"The evil genius is the one who walks daily with a smile over his grin."

"Lead by example and walk-through fire holding hands."

"Gone but never forgotten...forever in our hearts."

"The best kept secrets are your evil thoughts."

"A good game of chess, usually sets your opponent mind on fire, before checkmate."

"Making the enemy your friend, will destroy him."

"Don't feel sorry for me, I am as good as they come."

"Making the enemy your friend, will destroy him."

"Don't feel sorry for me, I am as good as they come."

"Don't let one mishap, change your view of the world."

"Keep your vows guarded, the thief comes at all times."

START DATE 7-11-16

Introduction

A strange looking old man sat inside Burger King. He was wearing a black three-piece suit and it appeared as if he was dressed for a funeral. The old man's black shoes had quite a few scuff marks. He ordered a large black coffee with no sugar, which was odd because people would normally prefer to have their cup of joe lite and sweet.

The snowflakes came down rapidly turning New Haven into a winter wonderland. The old man gazed out the holiday decorated windows and, directly across the street, there was a huge Catholic Church on the corner of Dixwell Avenue and Arch street. The old man started sipping his cup of coffee while keeping his eyes fixated on the church and the people entering it. Everyone seemed to be in the holiday spirits and all were dressed to impress. The women wore large feathered hats which caught snowflakes as they hurried up the snow-filled steps and entered through the massive wooden doors.

The streets and sidewalks were already blanketed with snow. Two large city plow trucks with yellow flashing lights drove back-to-back. One was clearing snow from the street while the other dropped grains of salt behind it in an effort to prevent accidents. Two New Haven police cruisers slowly drove by making the old man even more excited!

The old man glanced at his Timex wrist watch, he noticed that the date was December 25 and the time was 11:35 am. He then stood up from the table gulping down the last of his black coffee. While he was exiting, the young lady working the cash register observed that he was carrying a black bible by his side. He disappeared out of view...

Moments later, the church doors opened and the old man walked inside. As he slowly strolled down the aisle, he searched for a place to sit inside the crowded church. In the process he realized that quite a few ladies even had infants laying across their shoulder. The old man finally found an available seat next to a chubby old lady who smelled as if she bathed in perfume. She instructed her four young children sitting next to her to move closer together so that he would have space to sit. When the oldest of the four stuck his tongue out at the old lady, she waved one finger side to side in disapproval. The kid must have understood her sign language because he immediately slid over. The old man greeted the children with a smile, sat down, then placed his black classic fedora onto his lap.

He began staring straight ahead at a bald-headed white man standing behind the fancy pulpit wearing a white, black, and gold robe who was preaching the word of God. The preacher grasped everyone's full attention while instructing them to open their bibles to 1 Peter chapter 3 verse 10. Before the preacher began reading, he allowed them time to locate the scripture then said, "called to blessing". The church goers responded "Amen". The preacher then recited verse 10 down to the people – "He who would love life and see good days, let him refrain his tongue from evil, and his lips from speaking deceit. Let him turn away from evil and do good, let him seek peace and pursue it. For the eyes of the lord are on the righteous, and his ears are open to their prayers: But the face of the Lord is against those who do evil".

The old man glimpsed around and saw that the church goers were focused on the preacher. Soft voices could be heard quietly reading along. The old man stood up and placed his black King James Bible where he was seated. After positioning his fedora on top of his head, he then replied "pardon me" as he slid past the old lady and her children. Right when his hand reached out to grab the door handle, he overheard the preacher instructing everyone to "turn to Revelations Chapter 10", one of the children noticed that the old man left behind his bible so he looked up and around for him, however, the old man had already vanished. Once he traveled a distance away from the church, he decisively removed a black cell phone from his pocket and dialed 911 asking for the New Haven Police department. A female voice could be perceived on the other end asking the man, "is this an emergency sir?" The old man definitely replied "yes!" Informing the woman to listen carefully, **"you never get a second chance to make a good first impression"**

Without hesitation, he pressed the end button on his phone, his King James Bible made a loud beep, and then it viciously exploded!!! With extreme force, the entire church decimated into the air and left debris flying everywhere. In fact, the impact was so powerful its overturned vehicles in the rear parking lot and it also shattered the windows at Burger King. When the dark cloud of smoke eventually cleared away, a black stain remained, where the church once stood along with other burning rubble.

It wasn't until six years later that the city of New Haven had finally come back together after that dreadful day of the church explosion, which was considered by many to be one of the most atrocious incidents, the city had ever witnessed, the New Haven Police Department remained puzzled because they yet to have any persons of interest. The main concern for them keeping the phone call information confidential was to ensure that it was never divulged either to the public or to the news media on that wintery afternoon in December...

Chapter 1

Present Day

Two French Bull dogs were in the living room growling at each other which led to a fight over a bone. A male voice commanded Heaven and Hell to stop: both dogs paused, then scurried off in opposite directions. Sonny the brindle and fawn male, went underneath the couch while Cher, the brindle and white female, left out the room carrying the bone. Giving the pile of stale cigarette butts inside the ashtray and the fact that smoke often lingered in the air, a smoker definitely lived in the house, the television was showing a new sprint cell phone commercial which had been airing for about three months.

A smoldering cigarette butt was died out in the ashtray, a hand grabbed a white plastic sprint bag containing six I-phone boxes, then carried it out of the living room and down a flight of stairs into the basement. After a string was pulled, a bright light turned on revealing what appeared to be some kind of tool room. The bag was placed onto a metal table next to six remote control cars in which each car had their plastic covers removed exposing the miniature motors. Also, on the table were various sized screwdrivers, colorful spools of wire, and a black rubber and metal tipped pen used for soldering. Alongside of those items was a clump of some kind of gray clay. The table was set up as if an operation was about to occur. A pair of rubber latex surgical gloves were put on….

Hours later, all of the remote-control cars were placed into the bed of an old red Ford pickup truck. It was a beautiful day outside with plenty of sunshine. The old man glanced at his Timex wrist watch which displayed the time 3:05 pm then he muttered, "this should be a nice Toy Story" – his target today was Hartford Connecticut!

The Ford pickup truck exited the driveway and, while he was driving on the highway 91 north, a white Mercedes Benz GL450 truck came up from behind. He briefly looked over at the truck next to him and noticed a little white girl staring at him. She was sitting in a car seat with her finger in her nose so he decided to smile revealing his rotten teeth. The girl's eyes widened with fear.

The Benz truck sped past the pickup truck with its signal light blinking and veered off in a different direction towards Springfield Massachusetts.

He finally made it to Hartford but soon after found himself lost, so in an effort to obtain directions, he pulled into Ruper's gas station and rolled his window down beside a grey Acura TL. The Acura's tinted window lowered and Marijuana smoke quickly billowed out of the car. A short black dude with corn rows and wood framed Cartier eye glasses appeared and, when his mouth opened, the old man noticed a golden shine on three of his teeth. He then asked "what are you looking for old man"? The old man nervously responded, "sorry I am lost". Before the old man could say another word, the black dude in the passenger seat told Woodie to lean back, then picked up a chrome .45 caliber hand gun from his lap and pointed it at him. The Acura's tinted window went back up as the volume of the stereo was turned up.

The Acura exit the gas station onto Albany avenue passing Garden Street while the old man mumbled profanities and gave the Acura the middle finger. The old man exits the gas station as well and he slowly trailed behind the Acura and turned left onto Bedford street. His eyes lit up when he observed a bunch of children frolicking at a nearby park. Further down the street was a brick housing complex and which the old man, saw two girls getting inside the Acura. He watched it maneuver around a concrete barrier then make an illegal right-hand turn onto Mather street.

The old man slowly pulled over next to the park and, before he exited the truck, he scanned the area when he noticed that there was a church and free medical clinic across the street. There were children running around and getting wet under the sprinklers of the splash pad in an effort to cool down from the scorching summertime heat. He climbed out of his pickup then he grabbed the remote-control cars two at a time from the bed of his truck and, once the children noticed them, they raced over to him. To the children he exclaimed, "Enjoy"! With uncontrollable excitement, the children snatched them from him and ran away. He started to drive in the same direction as the Acura did, then he glanced one last time in his rearview mirror and saw two of them racing their remote-control cars in the street heading towards the housing complex.

Moments later, a petite dark-skinned woman came walking from the clinic, and she cut through the church parking lot onto Bedford Street. It seemed as if she was heading to the park and following closely behind her were four teenagers who were carrying flyers from the church. One of the teens tapped the woman on her shoulder in order to get her attention then he handed her a flyer. The four teens continued walking towards the housing complex passing out flyers along the way. The

3

woman peeked at the flyer which read 'Charity Dinner' then placed it inside her Coach handbag.

While at the park, the woman noticed her children in the distance playing with some remote-control cars so she approached them and asked, "where did you get those things from"?! The oldest replied, "some old white man gave them to us". The woman responded by insisting, "you better stop takin" stuff from strangers and be home by dark"!!! A silver Buick Lesabre pulled up alongside the woman as she walked towards the housing complex when a fair-complexioned bald dude rolled down his window and asked her to take a ride across town. So, she entered the vehicle, embraced the driver, then slowly drove off staring back at them.

The old man's Ford pickup truck was idling at the corner of Mather Street and Main Street when he grabbed his cell phone and dialed 911. The dispatcher answered, "911, what is your emergency"? After a short pause, the old man replied to her, **"Fear makes the wolf seem bigger than he is"**. Simultaneously, he pressed a small red button on a hand-held device while driving down Main Street and, all of a sudden, a massive explosion rocked Bedford Street!! Behind him, a giant black cloud of smoke formed a Hugh mushroom in the sky....

Chapter 2

First on the scene was Fox 61 News followed by the arrival of the Hartford Police Department and Fire Department. In an effort to corral the surging enormous crowd, the Police immediately installed yellow wooden 'DO NOT CROSS LINE' horses in three separate areas while the firemen quickly jumped off of their trucks and connected all necessary hoses to the water supplies.

Over the last hours, total chaos erupted along Bedford Street. The entire area was destroyed for it looked like 911 yet again – the brick housing complex that once stood was nothing but a massive pile of concrete and burning rubble. Next to appear was the American Red Cross who were ready to offer any medical assistance to all those in need and several officers combed through the crowd for information. From a distance, a bald-headed man could be seen escorting a familiar-looking petite woman towards the debacle who was frantically crying, screaming, and inquiring, 'where are my kids'?

The old man managed to reach home safely and he was now comfortably relaxing in his plush lazy boy recliner eating a bowl of buttered popcorn as if he was at the movies – the Featured Presentation today was, in fact, the Breaking News! He started tossing popcorn in the air and catching it in his mouth while intently listening to the female news reporter describe the severity of the explosion. He smirked with approval then he stood up and walked out of the living room with Sonny and Cher trailing behind him. He opens the back door and, as they bolted into the backyard, he realized just how much he had neglected it over the past couple of months. Disappearing into the unkept lawn and heading off in opposite directions, each dog had its own territory. One could be seen defecating with his head peering over the grass while the other must have been urinating because she was out of view. The old man shut the back door leaving them outside and he made his way to the bathroom.

For some strange reason, the old man grew accustomed to urinating while sitting down on the toilet. Needless to say, the old man's bathroom was far from the most sanitary. A pungent stench emanated from it, the tub was downright filthy, and the pulled back shower curtain exposed an insurmountable amount of mold and mildew that clung to all surfaces. While urinating, he thought to himself, 'the dogs might be hungry'. So, he left out of the bathroom without flushing the toilet and he decided to feed them. When the back door opened, the old man summoned them with a distinctive whistle so they came running towards him at full speed when he noticed that Cher had a sparrow dangling from her mouth. So, he promptly ordered, 'Drop It'! The bird immediately fell to the ground then the dogs proceeded inside in separate directions to their respective bowls. He grabbed the bird, shut the back door, then placed it inside his floor-standing freezer.

Now feeling an unyielding sense of power, the old man poured himself a celebratory double shot of Canadian Whiskey. He then carried the glass into the living room where he chugged it, slammed it on top of an oakwood stand, and collapsed into his recliner. He triumphantly lit a cigarette then his eyes zeroed in on the television which was still airing the Breaking News.

While a news camera was showing all the damage, he was responsible for, he took a drag from his cigarette and then he blew smoke circles at the screen. The ticker read: Millions of dollars, in damages and more than eighty dead so far.

The Fox 61 NEWS camera man rotated the camera to show four cadaver dogs just arrived on the scene who were released and began sniffing through concrete slabs searching for any survivors that might be trapped underneath. Then, three of the dogs started barking in different areas so, law enforcement and firemen rushed to them and they began removing heavy broken pieces of concrete in an effort to uncover bodies from the rubble. In disbelief, the veteran news reporter looked into the camera and she exclaimed, "the body count just keeps rising'!

The old man reached for his whiskey glass, realized it was empty, then he took one last deep drag from his camel cigarette and released smoke out of his nostrils and mouth with a look of victory written on his face. He doubted the authorities would ever apprehend him because, without no cooperation from the public, he believed that he was incapable of being defeated and he would remain at least one step ahead of them. On the television, the news report said, "if anyone has information please contact the Hartford Police Department" two phone numbers were displayed across the screen. The old man already had evil thoughts about how to top what happened in Hartford, however, he simply didn't have another location yet. He turned off the television then he proceeded into his bedroom.

The most noticeable objects in his bedroom were a large collection of vintage army memorabilia with a red, white, and blue poster of Uncle Sam hanging on the wall who was pointing his finger. The poster read, "I Want You" and it had several darts stuck into it mainly around his face. In addition, numerous sayings were hand-written all over the walls in which one of them read: **CHESS IS War Over The Board. The object is to crush the opponent's mind.** Another read: **A Good Scare Teaches More Than Good Advice.** It was obvious the old man had a Penchant for quotes. He began searching through a stack of porn DVD's until he found his favorite movie entitled 'Boot Camp Fuckers Vol. 1. He anxiously opened the DVD player and placed it inside. Feeling a little tipsy from the whiskey, he then reached for the remote control pressing the play button in the process and became comfortable enough looking at the TV screen with his uncircumcised penis in hand about to celebrate....

Chapter 3

Quantico, Virginia

Sarah Richardson, a beautiful Caucasian woman in her late forties was one of the best bomb specialist agents the F.B.I. has ever had. After an extensive career she was now retired from tracking down some of the most diabolical bombers the world has encountered. While out in the field back in 2006, she lost her partner Peter Holt who had to leave Sarah behind that day when attempting to apprehend their suspect Henry Dryer. The suspect eventually led Peter into a house that appeared to be abandoned, however it was actually lined with mirrors and a bomb lurked in the basement. Peter became trapped inside, but the suspect was able to exit, out the back door before detonating the bomb which blew the whole house up! Shards of glass flew everywhere.

At her partner Peter's funeral, Sarah was introduced to his wife and to their daughter and vowed to them she would bring Peter's killer to justice. Before embracing his family and departing, she walked up to the closed casket, looked at a much younger looking picture of him that stood on top, then said a silent prayer. Two years from the day Peter was laid to rest, Sarah and her new partner, a German Shepard K-9 dog named C.A.P. (Capture And Prosecute), were tipped off about his killer's where-abouts. She was informed that there were numerous satellite sightings of him in Russia, so, Sarah and her K-9 traveled there where they, after a long chase in the frigid cold, tracked him down. He ultimately met his fate in the mountains of Moscow with two 10mm slugs to the head.

At the F.B.I. facility, Sarah was now teaching Behavioral Analysis classes while Cap was working as a service dog for the blind. Her classroom of twelve always showed much respect for her because she took her job so seriously and when she spoke everyone remained silent making sure to not miss a single word. Each student had in front of them a folder labeled 'Profiler' and on the inside the folder contained more than thirty profiles of some of the most notorious criminals.

Sarah asked her students to open their folders and then she clicked on the projector machine – a picture of Ted Kowinski appeared on the large screen. She asked them, "Do you know who this person is?" While pointing to the picture with her stick, hands were raised into the air. She pointed her stick at a girl in the last row and said "you, young lady with the blond top knot?" The young lady slowly stood and stated, "Ted Kowinski AKA THE Unabomber". Sarah exclaimed "you are absolutely correct young lady". She then asked, "Does anyone know what his specialty was?" Again, several hands went up so she pointed at a young African American man in the front row who then confidently stood and blurred, "Mail bombs". Sarah smiled at him then said, "you are correct sir".

From there, Sarah instructed her students to turn the page while she clicked the button again. A photo of Timothy McVoigh was displayed so she yelled out, "Does anyone know who this person is?" Yet again, multiple hands shot up in the air. She pointed her stick towards the gentleman on the far right of the classroom who stood up and said, "Timothy McVoigh". Sarah said, "that is also correct". She walked around with her hands behind her back and, when she stopped, she asked the class, "what was his crime"? One more time, several hands raised. So, she pointed to a young lady sitting in an electric wheelchair who stated, "The Oklahoma Bombing". "You too are correct", Sarah responded.

Sarah told her students to turn the page. When an unknown man dressed in a navy-blue tailored Armani suit with his F.B.I. badge clipped to his lapel entered her classroom. He quickly apologized for the interruption then he whispered something into her ear. Sarah told her students, "class is dismissed". While everyone was closing their folders, she let them know that she might be gone for a while, and that, "there will be an exam on all the information contained in this folder when I return".

Two days later, Sarah was aboard a plane heading towards Bradley International Airport in Hartford Connecticut. In an effort to not disturb other passengers, she wore earbuds connected to her laptop as she watched video footage of the two previous devastating events that occurred in New Haven and Hartford. Analyzing the footage was her way of researching what she might possible be up against in the future.

Once her flight arrived, Sarah quickly traveled by Uber on her way to the Asylum Hill area and, as always, she performed a diligent investigation of that locale as well. From what she learned she knew the Governor lived close by and there was a centrally situated park that was perfect for her early morning jogs. Although the radio could barely be heard, she noticed that on 106.5 FM

'Dreams' by Fleetwood Mac was playing. The driver was attempting to strike up a conversation with her, however, she was simply too exhausted to respond to his inquiries but, she did, in fact, recognize the familiar yet desirable fragrance Arami Code Profumo he was wearing then she thought to herself, 'He smells fantastic, unfortunately he just isn't my type'. Considering she was always stationed in high-end homes by the Bureau, as expected, the Mercedes Benz Sprinter turned left onto Trautbrook street then pulled up to the front steps of a beautiful brick Brown Stone with a cobble stone circular driveway and a large well-manicured lawn. After carrying all of her leather designer luggage to the front door the driver was paid then he entered his vehicle and drove away listening to 'Runway' by Bon Jovi.

Sarah raised the brand-new welcome mat and retrieved two gold-colored keys then she wheeled her luggage behind her into the house. The chandelier was motion activated and it automatically lite up when she entered the house which was fully furnished with plenty of space, high ceiling, and hardwood floors with marble counter tops throughout – just the way she always requests. The only unknow to her was the vehicle that awaited in the garage. As she walked up the left side of the extravagant V-shaped stairwell, she yawned then headed towards the master bedroom. Sarah removed her black leather biker jacket, kicked off her black pumps, then collapsed into the enormous California King bed where she was swallowed by the plush mattress. Pulling the comforter over herself, she passed out within seconds....

Chapter 4

Sarah looked at the pink fit bit fastened around her wrist. When she made it back to the house from her morning jog at Elizabeth Park. She noticed quite a few stares out there when she was jogging. Sarah went into the bedroom and let her hair down which fell down to her lower back and inches from her buttock. She reached in to turn on the shower then touched the water with her hand to feel for the right temperature. She removed her tight Under Armour spandex suit. The bathroom slowly started to steam up as she unlatched her bra strap. When she bent over the spread of her derriere was enough to make any man's jaw drop. She stood up then tossed her matching panties to the side, her picture perfect hour glass figure was apparent. All her curves were impeccably shaped – especially for a woman her age.

Sarah stepped into the shower, letting the water hit her in the face. While she ran her fingers through her hair. She looked so relaxed lathering her taut and toned body. She turned around so the water could hit her backside and, at that moment, she thought about touching herself – that's how good the shower felt. Sarah knew that she better get out, before all hell broke loose and she could no longer control herself so, she stepped out wrapping her hair inside a towel. She grabbed another towel to dry off with, while she walked to the bedroom displaying the bareness of her backside and, with each step of the way, she left behind a trail of wet foot prints. Sarah entered the bedroom, then she stopped in front of a large mirror that was situated atop of a large Mahogany dresser. While she was drying off, she turned to her right side and in the mirror a small tattoo of Bruce Lee holding nunchus became visible on her rib cage. Nobody never ever saw her tattoo. To date, it was her best kept secret. Sarah idolized Brue Lee because of the way he handled himself in situations. Along with his diminutive size, wisdom and incredible strength. Sarah's favorite film was Enter the Dragon which explain the tattoo. She also took mixed martial art classes in college. Which inspired her to perform exercises, as meditation, and practice yoga.

Sarah got dressed then walk down the right side of the stairwell to bring the rest of her luggage into one of the other rooms. She exited that room carrying a Bruce Lee DVD box-set and her lap top. Sarah thought to herself, 'there's nothing wrong with a little Bruce Lee tonight'. She put the box-set on the kitchen counter then she placed her laptop on the long marble table. Sarah typed in her password while the computer was loading, she then glanced at her iPhone and saw a missed text message. So, she opened the message it read, 'How was the flight?' She sent back a happy face emoji and, seconds later, a reply appeared that read, 'Great!' After Sarah read the text, she walked away from her cell phone.

Going into the refrigerator, she grabbed a mineral water and an apple then she sat down in front of her laptop. She cut the apple into four slices then she clicked a small folder on the screen. And a page appeared that showed pictures and video footage from various news networks that were related to the bombings that took place in New Haven and Hartford. Sarah took a bite from one of her slices. While slowly looking at the pictures, one at a time, she tried to compare the damages to any of the profiles in her existing folder. She knew that there were millions of copy cats dying to make a name for themselves. Sarah had spent a few hours on the laptop studying all of the files. She sat in front of her laptop with a salad in front of her squeezing French dressing over it. Sarah replayed the video footage while she nibbled on her salad. She noticed a sun shower in view from the kitchen window, finished the salad, then closed the files. Once they all disappeared, she pressed the power button and closed the laptop. She grabbed her Bruce Lee box-set then she figured it was time to call it a night. Tomorrow, she had plans to visit the most recent bomb crime scene in Hartford. And, perhaps a few days later, she would probably take a trip to New Haven.

Sarah was still curious about what vehicle awaited her inside the garage so she opened the garage door and saw a beautiful dark blue Mercedes Benz SL550 coupe. Sarah shut the garage door with a smile on her face retired to her bedroom to catch up on some much-needed sleep. She put on something more comfortable then she took Enter the Dragon out and placed it inside the DVD player. She laid back underneath the comforter, pressed play, then began watching her favorite movie. She felt her eye lids getting heavy hallway through the movie and eventually dozed off. When she finally opened her eyes, Bruce Lee had deep lacerations on his face, chest, and stomach from fighting a man with an interchangeable knifed hand inside a glass room. To her dismay, Sarah realized she had slept through almost the entire movie. She watched the rest of it, grabbed her pillow, and then turned over onto her side. By the time the film credits appeared, she pressed the power button and, once again, fell into a deep sleep....

Chapter 5

In preparation for her journey to the crime scene at the north end of Hartford, Sarah was getting dressed in her bedroom while speaking with Robert Whirlwind a colleague of hers who was stationed at F.B.I facility (headquarters) in Washington DC. Sarah iPhone laid on the dresser and set to speakerphone, she moved freely about as they conversed regarding the benefits of the most up-to-date technology incorporated inside her new Mercedes Benz.

First and likely the most beneficial, a pair of eye glasses that sat inside the glove compartment which were capable of detecting where bombs were detonated and an additional hologram feature that brought back images of where buildings existed. He also stated that everything she views through this eyewear is being recorded and stored on a flash drive so that it could be played back at a later time. Secondly, was a clear state-of-the-art drone that sat inside the trunk Headquarters code-named it 'Casper the friendly Ghost' due to its 360° view finder that was capable of zooming in on an ant mile away. Casper was so small and transparent the human eye could barely notice it.

Robert asked Sarah if she had ever seen the TV show 'Person of interest'. She replied no. So, he explained to her, on that show, everyone and everything can be a target. She exclaimed, Great! She figured she could use any help offered in order to catch this sick bastard. Their phone call ended then Sarah tied up her

New Balance sneakers before standing in front of the dresser mirror and configuring her hair into a 'top knot'. Reaching for the iPhone and grabbing her Dior sunglasses, she left the bedroom and sauntered down the stair well and into the living room. She stopped at a large bookshelf where she glanced at the title of a book there called 'V is for Vengeance' by Sue Grafton. She recalled hearing the book received phenomenal reviews. As she walked away heading towards the kitchen, she asked her amazon device, "what was the weather like?" Alexa responded, "80° degrees today with plenty of sunshine". Sarah took a bite out the apple then she heard some children laughing so, she peeked out the kitchen blinds. She saw a lady spraying them with a water hose while they frolicked in the back yard. Sarah then asked Alexa for the time Alexa replied, "2:36 PM".

She grabbed a bottle of spring water out the refrigerator then exited the door towards the garage. Moments later, the garage door opened slowly. Through voice activation, Sarah engaged her GPS system. Destination: Albany Avenue and Bedford street. She glanced at herself in the rear-view mirror while placing her sun glasses over her eyes. The dark blue Mercedes Benz SL550 pulled out and glistened in the sun. Following the navigation's direction, she drove away with the windows up. Taking full advantage of her vehicle's air conditioning system. She noticed a plethora of neighbors who were outside enjoying the beautiful weather. Heads turned as she drove by and, 15 minutes later, the GPS said. "you have arrived to destination". She pulled the coupe to the curb and examined the street signs. Before she exited the vehicle, she stared at a deserted area where numerous candles could be seen along with balloons and other religious items. An entire block was wiped out and decimated. She said a quick prayer for all the lost lives, took off her shades, then replaced them with her federally issued eye glasses from the glove compartment.

Sarah stood on the corner of Albany Avenue and Bedford Street and once again, noticed that the destruction was close to one of the worst she'd ever witnessed. She ambled from Garden Street then walked right through the concrete and dirt onto Bedford Street. Looking at the ground the whole time, she saw eight candles, numerous stuffed animals, and some circular shaped objects scattered all around. Sarah reached down to pick up one of the objects which appeared to be a button containing a picture of a teenager with his name and the words – Rest In Peace printed on it. As she walked back to the beginning of the block, she felt ready to try out the hologram feature on her eye glasses. So, she touched a button on the side of them. And, almost magically, the empty block became full of the previously missing edifices – she couldn't believe her eyes for all that was missing now had reappeared. She was astonished how the block use to look. Sarah stood on the left side of Bedford Street where the back of the free clinic and the Y.M.C.A could be seen across the street. When she started walking in the middle of the street buildings were reappearing – the back of the church, Brook Street Park and the Brick housing complex!

Sarah presses another button and six fluorescent green stains could be seen in different areas on both sides of the street. The green glow indicated where the bombs had been detonated. There were four at the park and two down near the brick housing complex. She pondered why were the explosions in various locations? She then inquired to herself, 'could they had been inside of something? She continued to walk to the end of the block then looked through a gap in the landscape onto Mather Street. She slowly turned around doing a 360-degree movement so she could video record everything on the empty torn-down block. When she removed her high-tech eye wear, the entire block looked like a scene from a Mad Max movie – yellow strips of police caution tape laid all around on the ground. Sarah wiped the sweat away from her forehead.

When Sarah returned to her vehicle, a slim dark-skinned woman carrying a plastic shopping bag approached her and introduced herself as Bernice. Bernice claimed that her four children perished there. Sarah quickly recognized Bernice's T-shirt which read "Rest in Peace" with four adorable faces surrounded by clouds to indicate Heaven. They shook hands then Bernice retorted, "she might have some useful information". So, Sarah placed the special eye-wear back on and Bernice started telling her all that she could possibly remember. She began with when she came out the free clinic and was walking around the corner onto Bedford Street towards the park to checkup on her children. Four teens were walking behind them one handed me a flyer. They went walking down the street passing out more flyers along the way. Also, when she reached her children, they were playing with some yellow & black remote-control cars. She asked them, "where did they get them from?' So, the oldest one replied, "A old white man gave them the cars". After that, she walked down the street towards the brick apartments where she saw two kids playing with what appeared to be the same remote-control cars. Bernice added that her friend, then pulled up to her in his vehicle and asked her to take a ride. So, she entered the car and they drove across town, only to return home to her worst night-mare. Tears began rolling down Bernice's face – Sarah embraced her. Before thanking her for all of the valuable information. She handed Bernice a business card and told her to please feel free to call her, if she remembers anything else. Bernice glanced at the card which read F.B.I. Special Bomb Unit, Sarah Richardson along with two phone numbers at the bottom. She walked towards the location of where the park once stood and placed four teddy bears on the ground.

Sarah entered her vehicle with a vengeful scowl on her face. Then, inserted the special eye back into the glove compartment, she then reached for her sunglasses. Sarah took one last look at Bernice who was kissing the ground, where her four children last played then drove away and headed back home. On her way there, she was craving some Chinese food. So, the GPS lead her down the street in that direction. Sarah ordered her food then left out the Chinese restaurant carrying a small bag. Just as she was getting inside the car, two women walked by and told her that she has a beautiful car. Sarah smiled then said, "thank you – very much" to the women, while shutting the car door. She drove the rest of the way with the smell of Chinese food permeating the cabin of her vehicle through the bag. And, ten minutes later, she pulled into the garage. Sarah exited the vehicle, opened the door, walked inside her home, and then she stood at the kitchen counter removing four egg rolls, a plastic container full of watermelon chunks, and two fortune cookies out the bag.

Sarah devoured her food while contemplating what Bernice had told her. Now, she realized the bombs could have been planted inside those remote-control cars. That information Bernice had provided was a major breakthrough – the bomber specialized in placing hidden explosives into small objects. Sarah broke open one of her fortune cookies which read: **The first step to solving any problem is to begin.** She broke opened the last cookie and that one read: **What's done in the dark, soon comes to light.** Sarah wiped the counter clean thinking to herself, "Absolutely!" Then she walked into the living room and headed to the bookshelf then grabbed a hard cover book titled 'V is for Vengeance'. She turned the book over so she could read the blurb. She smiled wryly then headed up the stair well with the book in hand….

Chapter 6

Sarah woke up early and, for some reason, she couldn't stop thinking about that sick bastard! She was unable to fall back asleep so she sat in front of her laptop and searched online for toy stores within a fifty-mile radius in hopes that the information Bernice provided could be useful in obtaining solid leads as to who might be responsible for the bombings. A list of possible toy stores appeared on the screen. So, she started scrolling down for the closest ones. She clicked on the Toys R US site then typed in remote-control cars in the search box. Numerous remote-control cars of various styles, sizes, and costs were displayed on the screen. She researched every single one that store made available for purchase however none of them seemed to match the correct description. She decided to save about ten different pictures of cars for future reference.

A few hours later, Sarah Finally got dressed, then she went downstairs and headed into the kitchen. She was wearing a Yale baseball cap with her long ponytail protruding out the back. She opened the refrigerator door and noticed that there was only one bottle of water left. So, she grabbed it and her left-over container of watermelon. She then took a peek out of her kitchen blinds and saw her neighbor assembling a large blue and white circular above ground pool. She stuck her fork into the last piece of watermelon, looked inside the container, acknowledged the puddle of juice at the bottom, then she tilted the container back and savored that sweet juice!

Sarah remembered Walgreens had a sale on cases of bottled water for half price. So, she decided to drive there. She loved her water for it was the best thing to have around the house especially when the weather was scorching hot! Sarah pulled into the Walgreens parking lot, parked in between a late model BMW5-seriees and Mazda CX-9, then when she exited her vehicle, she became startled by the high-pitched barks of two cute little shih Tzu's. The dogs were trying to stick their small heads, through the crack in the window until this skinny Caucasian woman carrying a Louis Vuitton Bumbag on her shoulder. Approached the BMW with two plastic Walgreen bags in her hand. She ordered both of them to "hush" and they became quiet although their tails continued to wag.

Sarah walked through the sliding glass door and grabbed a Walgreen's discount flyer, then she picked up a red basket by the handles. She headed directly to the feminine hygiene aisle to pick up a few items. After that, while she was making her way to the bottled water section, she stumbled upon a toy aisle. So, instead, she began walking down that aisle and when she got half-way down it, she encountered a bunch of black and yellow remote-control cars priced at $19.99. Sarah immediately wondered, 'could these be the same remote-control cars?' then she promptly asked a store clerk if she could speak with the manager. Young black petite lady soon appeared, she inquired to Sarah, "how may I help you miss?" Sarah put down the basket, displaying her items which included a box of tampons, a bottle of skin lotion and a vinegar and water disposable douche. She brandished her F.B.I. badge then glanced at the young lady's name tag so, Sarah told 'Tammy' she needed to review the surveillance tapes from the last few months because she wanted to see who bought remote-control cars within that time frame. She handed Tammy a card and Tammy was amazed that she actually met a federal agent. Tammy took the card then said, "I will get right on it Ms. Richardson". She quickly walked away then disappeared through the 'employee's only' door. When Sarah was ready to check out at the register, she politely asked one of the employees to grab her two cases of Poland Spring bottled water, she paid for her items, then left the store.

Sarah made it back to the house and carried both cases of water with a plastic Walgreens bag on top inside the house. She stacked twelve bottles of water in the refrigerator, took a look through the blinds and saw that her neighbor finally put the pool together and it was currently filling with water. A large blown-up plastic swan and four life jackets were laid on the grass. Sarah smiled then walked away from the window. She passed through the living room with the Walgreens' bag in hand. She asked Alexa what is the time? Alexa replied, "11:25am".

Sarah was sitting on the edge of her bed and she was relaying to Robert Whirlwind on the phone all the information she had just received. She asked him, "could Casper scan a picture for me?" Robert said, "absolutely it's called facial recognition". He began telling Sarah that once Casper found a match it will automatically display live video footage of the suspect's location. This was precisely just what Sarah wanted to hear. So, she thanked Robert for the information before they ended their phone conversation.

Two hours later, Sarah received a call from Tammy who sounded excited! She informed Sarah she was able to retrieve the video footage that she had requested. Sarah replied, "I am on my way". When Sarah walked into the kitchen, she heard water splashing and kids laughing. She left out the door getting inside her vehicle and, minutes later, she arrived at Walgreens. As she walked toward the entrance, a foul odor of cigarette smoke ran through her nostrils. While she made eye contact with a peculiar looking old white man with a long beard. She walked inside and he headed towards an old red Ford F150 pickup truck. Sarah was greeted by Tammy then she was escorted upstairs into a room with a two-sided mirror overlooking the store. Sarah looked down and watched people browsing around the store and shopping. She saw a male employee who was busy stacking shelves. When a white lady walked behind him, she stuffed merchandise from another aisle inside her large black bag. So, Tammy called down to the front desk and told the security guard to apprehend her. Tammy mentioned to Sarah that at least four or five people get caught stealing each shift. Tammy sat in front of the monitor while Sarah stood right directly behind her and both of them watched intently. They watched from several camera angles on the monitor. Then finally some man in an electric wheel chair could be seen balancing four remote control cars in his lap while a store employee carried two more for him. Sarah asked Tammy, "can you zoom in?" Sarah noticed the man was an amputee, she told Tammy to zoom closer on his facial features. Sarah noticed that he had scars on his face and that his lip was disfigured. She asked Tammy could she zoom any closer the man whole face quickly took over the monitor. Sarah stared him in the eyes, as if she seen them before however, she just wasn't sure where. Sarah's next move was to see how the remote-control cars were paid for. She hoped it was done by credit card because she would then be able to get an address. Unfortunately, it wasn't the case – the man paid with cash.

Sarah asked Tammy to contact that employee who was carrying the two cars for the man. Because she would like to ask him, a few questions. Tammy looked at the employees work schedules. Then she stated, "Jerome should be here any minute" and Tammy was correct because literally one minute later, he walked through the automated sliding door. She called him on the intercom and told him to come up to the office. When Jerome got upstairs Sarah showed him her badge and told him that she would like to ask him a few questions about this man. She pointed to the monitor and, when Jerome looked at it, he couldn't help but remember the man in the electric wheel chair. Jerome said, "he didn't talk much but he had a pungent smell to him, like stale cigarettes". Sarah asked him if he helped by bringing the toys to his vehicle. Jerome said, "he did offer to help". However, the man replied, "No thank you" and left out the store. Sarah turned to Tammy then asked her to print two copies of the man – first one a full body shot and the second a close-up of his face. Sarah gave Jerome one of her contact cards and explained to him that the man might be considered dangerous. So, be extremely cautious in his presence. If he comes back please try to obtain a description of his vehicle and, if possible, his plate number.

Tammy was looking through the mirror and saw a woman who was pushing a baby carriage. She stopped and was looking down, when her toddler reached out and knocked two jars of jelly off the shelf onto the floor. The woman tapped the toddler on the hand then she pushed the carriage down the aisle and away from the mess. Tammy shook her head side to side in disgust, then she instructed Jerome to go clean it. Before someone slips and get cut by the glass on aisle 5. Sarah shook his hand then he exited the door and down the steps to search for the mop bucket and a wet floor sign....

Chapter 7

After she dressed, Sarah stood in front of the mirror to check herself out. She wore dark blue slacks and a matching blazer, a crisp white button up shirt, and as usual a Glock 9 underneath her attire – clearly looking like Special F.B.I agent Sarah Richardson today. Her badge was visible on her waist line and on her feet were some black leather flats. Placing her designer sunglasses over her eyes, Sarah left the house and traveled to the Hartford Police Department where she had a 10:00 am meeting scheduled with the chief of police.

Once there, she shared some information about the bomber and she was ready to get Connecticut involved. The only thing she was hesitant to divulge the suspect's identity for she felt that anything could go wrong such as the suspect attempting to flee the state. All things considered; Sarah believed he was hardly a thoroughbred like the other ones. But she simply wasn't willing to chance it either. She remained confident as she started to think to herself was, he an individual who couldn't have his way or perhaps he was bullied at some point in his life and decided to take it out on innocent people. If so, he was a coward. The Police Department door opened, Sarah and the chief walked out and stood in front of both the news media and the families and friends of the victims – everybody was seeking answers.... The Police chief stood in front with his fellow subordinates behind him and Sarah was standing not too far away, but a little off to the right of them. For she was more of a 'behind the scene' kind of agent. From her perspective, she could care less about the spot light. Sarah tended to make her presence known only once the perpetrator was finally captured.

The chief began his speech putting everyone on 'High Alert' by first stating that they have some incredible leads regarding what has been happening and, also, who might be the person responsible for these horrific events. He told the people, "If you see something, say something and please do not take anything from strangers. If you find something in the streets do not touch it, leave it and, call the Police Department". The news media's cameras were flashing as if they were positioned along a Red-Carpet Runway event and a plethora of voice recorders were held high and pointed towards the chief of Police. He finally asked "does anyone have questions?" Several hands were raised so, he pointed to the lady holding the News 8 microphone. She asked, "Do they know either the race or age of the bomber?" He replied, "not at this time but he is a male".

Then added, "next question please?" He pointed to the lady with an NBC microphone who asked, "is there anything in particular he's looking for?" The chief said, "from what I can ascertain the bomber has been aiming for soft targets, meaning places where large amounts of people will accumulate". He then concluded, "this is the last question". He pointed to the man from Fox 61 news who posed a valid inquiry, question, "is there going to be extra security for all schools?" The chief quickly responded, "Absolutely!" Then he waved his hand saying "Thank you!!!" The gathering of officers parted ways like Moses did the Red Sea and then they all followed the chief back inside headquarters. Sarah had disappeared ten minutes before....

Chapter 8

Sarah was on her sixth lap around the park jogging at a steady pace, when her cell phone rang, so, she slowed down after passing two women pushing strollers. While stationary, Sarah press a small button on her hands-free headset and said, "hello" as she sweat from her brow. On the other end a voice replied, "good morning, Tammy". Tammy seemed overwhelmed, when she began informing Sarah that she has both the parking lot surveillance footage and a description of the vehicle in question pointing out that it was a handicapped accessible van. Due to the fact, the man entered through an electric side door elevated and platform. When the vehicle drove away, the surveillance camera was able to catch a glimpse of his license plate. Based on Tammy's adept inclinations, Sarah avowed to Tammy that she would be an excellent law enforcement officer. Tammy's smile extended from ear to ear for she always had an affinity to become a Police Officer. Every since her high school years, she loved to read True Crime novels and her favorite author was Ann Rule. If Tammy could help in any kind of way, she would gladly do so. Before they hung up, Sarah thanked Tammy again for her cooperation and assistance then told her she'll be there in about an hour.

To prevent cooling off, Sarah returned to her workout and commenced her jog again. While thinking about how helpful Tammy had become. She caught up with and passed by the two ladies pushing the strollers. Moments later, she also noticed an older man with a plastic bag over his hand who was picking up after his dog. So, she briefly smiled as she passed them by. After easily completing ten laps, she exited the park and headed back home to shower up and begin her day.

Sarah's blue Mercedes Coupe pulled into the Walgreens parking lot and Jerome immediately spotted it as the car drove by and parked on the left side of the entrance. Sarah exited the vehicle, took her shades off, then placed them inside her jacket's inner pocket. She noticed Jerome getting out the passenger side of a blue Toyota Camry, walk to the driver's side, then give an attractive young lady a kiss on her lips. Then he waved at her and a baby sitting inside a car seat and placed his Walgreen's name tag on his shirt, while walking into the store just moments after Sarah. He caught up to her to compliment the Mercedes Benz which was one of his dream cars. Always the gentlemen, Jerome held the door that leads upstairs to the control room open for Sarah, then punched in on the clock. While Sarah greeted Tammy with a firm handshake. Tammy was all smiles sitting in front of the monitor with Sarah standing behind her and looking at the screen. They both observed the man press a button on his key and the side door on his van opened to display a ramp. He rode up the ramp on his electric wheelchair and as the door was closing, he could be seen tossing the Walgreen bags into the back. The van begins backing out – the man was behind the steering wheel turned around so he could properly exit the parking lot. Tammy paused the tape then zoomed in on his license plate, while pointing to a pen and pad for Sarah to write down the make, model, and plate number of the van alas! Sarah glanced at Tammy then gave her a 'high five' Sarah left the store got inside her car, then sat behind the wheel to relay to Robert the information she just received from Tammy.

Before Sarah reached home, Robert had already returned her call to inform her that he got some valid information as to the man's identity. His name is Randall Goldberg, 44 years of age, an army veteran who was discharged after an unfortunate encounter with a suicide bomber in Afghanistan. As a result, he lost his left leg. Randy's driver license photo shows him with a cleanly shaven face and some permanent facial scars around his left cheek and jaw bone which may indicate he's also missing a few teeth. His address was 9 Windsor Rd, Hamden, CT. So, Robert was about to contact the Hamden Police Department. So, they could put the house under surveillance until the bomb specialist arrived. Robert instructed Sarah to approach with extreme caution before hanging up the phone. Sarah left out the Kitchen walking through the living room into one of the first-floor rooms. Then she opened a silver attaché case which housed six different automatic handguns inside it. She grabbed her favorite, a light-weight Glock 9, inserted a magazine, then cocked it back to put a bullet into the chamber. Latching the safety mechanism first, she tucked the fire-arm inside her waistband then clipped her F.B.I. badge to her belt and scampered out the house. She waited in her vehicle for the garage door to open as she pulled the brim of her baseball cap down and her shades over her eyes, she exited the garage. While listening intently to the navigation system directing her to the highway and toward her destination.

The Hamden Police Department had been planning for the raid so they rushed over to the address without missing a beat and in the process, disobeyed the direct order they were given by the F.B.I. Six police cruisers were parked out front of a white cape with a detached one car garage while several officers wearing tactical gear moved around to the back of the house to properly set up and, two minutes later, the front door was breached and thus knocked off its hinges as officers rushed inside with assault weapons drawn. A revolting stench quickly caught the men off guard so they were forced to cover their noses from the pungent odor. In fact, their stomachs irrevocably turned causing some to project vomit. The house was dark, devoid of furnishings, and appeared to have been vacant for quite some time. Flies could be heard buzzing throughout and the only source of light was from the flashlights attached to the assault weapons.

Inside the master bedroom, the wall paint was peeling badly and there was writing all over the walls which seemed to be various quotes written in dried-up blood. One of the quotes read, **"A friend is someone who understands your past, believes in your future, and accepts you just the way you are"**. Once each room was secured a voice yelled out "clear!" The bathroom mirror was shattered with another quote emblazoned, **"Death is only a crossing over into another world"**. A voice could be heard shouting "this is one deranged individual we are dealing with!" The toilet was full of decrepit and dried feces and the bathtub had rings of dirt circling around its walls. The officers all lined up strategically to head down to the basement. Once there, officers stepped over mice that were running in and out of old holes when the lead officer, noticed a dead bolted door. So, he waved his hand to order the officer carrying the batter ram to move forward. A next officer counted aloud, "three, two, one!" Then the batter ram pounded the door it swung open triggering a perimeter switch and the entire house was rocked by a destructive force decimating everybody and everything into pieces! The house was fully consumed with a small portion of the garage still in flames and small wooden pieces of debris burned in and around the street.

By the time Sarah arrived, the Fire Department had just finished putting out the fires. The only remnants were a bunch of smoke in the air and the smell of charred wood that surrounded on explosion mark where the house once stood. Sarah closely observed the crowd of onlookers some of which were communicating with the news media. Sarah was standing next to an elderly woman who stated, "the house has been empty for at least three or four years now". Sarah spotted Hamden Police Chief so she moved her way through the crowd and stopped near the chief who was sobbing inside his cruiser with the door open. Sarah knelt down in front of him then inquired, "how many of your men did you lose?" The chief replied," Twelve of his best including his eldest son". His son was the one who had taken the phone call from F.B.I. agent Robert Whirlwind. The chief recognized Sarah's F.B.I badge – Special bomb unit. Then he said, "My son was supposed to wait for you". Sarah just shook her head in disappointment for she had nothing more to offer – She was at a loss for words. She turned to look at where the house once stood and then thought to herself, "your days are numbered Goldberg!" She walked closer to the site while she watched a female officer install yellow 'Police line do not cross' tape around the area. Sarah could smell a certain kind of chemical in the air and immediately said," a C-4 explosive was used". She put on her special eyewear, pressed the button and a hologram image of the house reappeared. Sarah scanned the house and a fluorescent green spot could be seen in the basement which indicated the location of the blast's origin. Sarah removed those eyeglasses walked back over to the chief, consoled him with a warm heartfelt embrace, then whispered in his ear "I will get this son of a bitch!" She patted the chief on his shoulder then slowly walked through the crowd and climbed into her car. She sat there inside while contemplating the possibility that she too might would have disintegrated into thin air if they would have followed the direct order. However, that was not to be for she was still alive for a reason and that purpose was to capture this sick handicapped bastard! Determined, she started the car and drove off....

Chapter 9

Sergeant Fred Jackson yelled out to a young Randy Goldberg. "Boy you are not done yet!" Reluctantly, Randy dropped off of his bunk. He was literally sleeping while standing and thoroughly exhausted after an arduous day of both slow marches and hiking with heavy backpacks and who would have thought that basic training was easy? It was in fact, the most extreme and challenging form of training known throughout the world – both mentally and physically. Randy had finally come to his senses when an ice-cold bucket of water fell on him. He stood stiff at attention and replied, "yes sir!" As he saluted the sergeant. All of the service men began cackling out loud making Randy the laughing stock of the barracks. He was ordered to clean pots, scrub toilets, and 'spit shine' boots and, when noontime came, Randy and three other cadets spent the rest of the day performing meaningless and frivolous tasks like building rock pyramids amid the sweltering head.

Six months had gone by; Randy and a fellow cadet name Jason Wells AKA 'Candy man' were unexpectedly deployed to Afghanistan on Special assignment. The day after arriving they were taken on a tour around the base while being introduced to numerous soldiers of all ethnicities – it seemed to, 'break the ice' so to speak Randy then noticed that everyone spoke highly of a particular U.S. Navy Seal named Christopher Kyle. They emulated him so much you would have thought he was a deity well in some sense, he was for Chris was acknowledged as having the most career sniper kills in U.S. military history. Although, it was confirmed that he had more than 150 kills, some people argued that he had many more under his belt. Randy insisted he himself was not a coward. Despite the fact that, he took on an imaginary 'tough guy' persona. He stated by the time his term in the army was over people would be talking about him as the man who blew everything up!

Randy and Jason had become members of the elite 3-33 Infantry Battalion known as the "crash crew". The two were inseparable and it seemed like where ever one went the other followed. Randy and Jason developed a brotherly bond that could not be severed. Randy was the one who handled the explosives by planting IED bombs in the ground and deep out around the perimeter of the base which would reduce the chances of sneak attacks on ground. Although, Randy could turn anything into a bomb, he was still labeled the butt end of all jokes however, many people did not laugh as much as or as often as before. Perhaps, because of his new nickname 'Dr. Boom'. Randy was now considered as having a successful military career.

An entire year had transpired, although, the heat was scorching, everyone had become acclimated to it. Randy, Candy Man, and four other soldiers were handpicked to ride into a small town. The Platoon leader named 'Black Cloud' told everyone they would be gone for about two or three days. He concluded by making everyone laugh with, "everyone should come back in one piece except Dr. Boom". Candyman patted Randy on his helmet saying, "it was only a joke". They climbed into the tank and proceeded accordingly while a Humvee followed behind them – The crew always traveled with no less than two vehicles following each other. Hours en route had passed by and they started seeing a bunch of bullets – riddled concrete buildings and quite a few areas were ablaze. Somewhere in the far away distance, harrowing sounds of gun fire and explosions could be heard. The two vehicles were unstoppable traversing over all kinds of rough terrain in their paths. They were now definitely behind enemy lines so everyone sat quietly with hands clutching their assault weapons. Black Cloud instructed all occupants of the tank to be wary for he needed their eyes and ears, because the territory they were encroaching on was called Hell on Earth.

Once there, the luminous skies emitted extraordinary colors – more like crimson reds and dark oranges. The tank had finally come to a halt. Candyman relayed to Black Cloud that there were children blocking the road. Black Cloud replied," let off a shot, they'll run away". Candyman let off a shot from his assault rifle however, he reported back that they didn't acknowledge the gun fire. The kids just continued to hold hands while rotating and frolicking in circles. Randy was ordered to exit the tank so he could remove the kids from the dirt road. The latch opened on the tank and Randy hopped down then walked cautiously towards the kids. He ordered them to move off the road but they ignored him and had now formed a complete circle around him. He thought to himself, "were they high on opium". Then, all of a sudden, one of them grabbed Randy by his left leg while the others scattered swiftly in opposite directions.

Randy frantically pushed the kid away however the kid held on tightly and began yelling out "Allah U Akbar!" Instantaneously the boy pressed a button on his chest, a flash of light had appeared, then Randy's body was blown upward off his feet and into the air only to land nearly twenty feet away from where he was standing. Sand and grit covered his face and his ears were ringing loudly. He glimpsed down at his lower body and something neither appealed nor felt right to him. Candyman was the first to exit the tank while calling out to Randy, aiming his assault weapon, and firing random shots. Black Cloud was next out ordering Candyman to 'cease fire!' Everyone was now out of both vehicles and the crash crew had formed a circle in order to protect one another as they made way over towards Randy who might be badly injured and Candyman. Just as the crew reached them, enemy fire began to whizz past while Randy was being dragged away. The crash crew immediately returned fire; however, Randy had already blacked out by this time. The opposition was attempting to move closer to obtain better shots. The crash crew could literally smell their acrid sweat from beyond the trenches as they, let off multiple shots and threw grenades in a desperate effort to force the enemy to retreat. They were eventually able to make it back into the tank and then destroy everything in the surrounding area.

Hours later, Randy awoke on a cot in a field hospital with five medics working on him, near his left leg and, as fast as blood was transfused into him, it leaked out rendering him very weak and light headed. He tried to focus down in that direction but when his eyes zoomed in, he gazed from the foot up and unfortunately his appendage was missing! One of the medics stated, "he's awake" and, soon there after that, Randy passed out again. The rescue chopper arrived so Candyman helped carry Randy onto the chopper. Weeks later, Randy's Platoon was transferred out. The next time Randy opened his eyes, he was uncertain of his whereabouts his brain simply couldn't register the location for he was completely shell-shocked.

Months had transpired since the surgery and Randy was now at the Bethesda Maryland Naval Medical Center outside D.C. Randy's left leg had been amputated just below the knee and the excruciating pain in the nub of his leg was so severe that even the flutter of air when doctors walked past would make him scream in agony. The intravenously-fed drip of morphine had side effects which caused intense nausea and prolonged periods of vomiting and, eventually, his body developed a suppressed immune response to them. One day, he eased his left leg out of his hospital gown, held his limb up with his hand, and he was at a loss for words for his whole life would be changed indefinitely. He still had yet to build up the courage to even look into a mirror and reveal the indelible images of scars he will be forced to contend with forever. Randy's dream of receiving a medal of honor was now shattered.

He was finally moved to a rehab clinic where he was about to get fitted for a prosthetic leg and, once again, relearn how to walk. Randy was introduced to so many other seriously wounded soldiers it seemed like a freak show. Being introduced to them might have been the worst thing to happen to him because everyone had derogatory commentary about this rehabilitation facility, Randy felt a level of discomfort unlike anything he had ever previously experienced. Everyone had lost hope for if they were no longer fighting for this country, they were no longer of use – just wastes of both skin and time. Randy managed to be friend; a black heavy-set ex-soldier named Barry Johnson who was fortunate to survive a point-blank range head shot! Once his cranium was reconstructed, he slowly began to heal. Because of this the staff affectionately named him 'Iron Man'. Barry had been recuperating there for quite some time, and would soon be released. When they were granted recess outside for some much-needed fresh air and sunshine, and, without exception, Barry and Randy would always sit together. Randy would be subjected to listening to Barry reiterate the same stories to him time and time again about a record deal he once had and a double-wide trailer he possessed in upstate New York (Buffalo).

Once the men were brought back inside it felt like they were forced to contend with a living hell once more. The area where the wounded soldiers were housed had an offensively unpleasant smell which was something similar to an outhouse kept indoors that is constantly being used with the door left wide open! One day, the food upset his stomach so badly he had diarrhea and soiled himself shortly afterwards, however, it took the entire day for an orderly to come around to clean him. The nurses were lazy and, truthfully speaking, had no interest in changing grown men whether handicapped or not. This added to the soldier's feelings of helplessness and unworthiness. A few of the guys including Barry used to even act inappropriately with the orderlies, and, every so often, a soldier would be fortunate enough to convince a nurse to either perform fellatio or execute an oiled, gloved manual release on them only to eventually break his promise of secrecy. The end result for the orderly would be having to be walked out of the hospital fully disgraced in handcuffs, which really shouldn't have triggered them to not do their jobs or not. Everything about the facility had become a mystery to Randy. Especially considering this particular one had one of the highest suicide rates in the country – more than a dozen soldiers committed suicide after discharging from service. A few green Beret combat medics had arrived to keep the majority of the soldiers constantly sedated. Randy couldn't deal with anymore of those stories for they were beginning to drive him crazy. He already had to contend with the unavoidable truth that he was in-advertently becoming a soldier who endured a life – changing experience of not leaving the service the same way he entered.

The last Sunday of each month they began doing karaoke and Barry would always steal the show by singing 'just the way you are' by his namesake Barry White. His sonorous voice was enough to make every female nurse dripping wet between their legs during his performances. If they were at a live concert their panties would invariably be tossed on stage. By the time Barry finished singing, Randy started to believe the stories he always felt compelled to tell. Later that night, Barry showed Randy a little secret by pulling out several pair of lace panties from his hidden cache; Randy sat back in his wheelchair and smiled. Randy knew Barry was far from mentally stable, but perhaps not nearly as bad as some of the others. Unexpectedly, while Randy was in morning therapy, Barry had been discharged! Fortunately, Barry left a Buffalo, New York address behind for him.

Two years had gone by Randy was now able to walk around on his prosthetic leg albeit with the help of a cane for he was determined to walk again. Randy had exchanged information with outside speaker Michael Walker who was a Spiritual man committed to helping wounded warriors. Randy's discharge date was coming in a few weeks, and, for the first time, he received a distressing phone call that his mother had passed away from cancer. Because of this, Randy was discharged one week early and Michael was, as promised, waiting outside in his mud-laden Toyota Land Cruiser to give him a lift. Michael was listening to 'Born in the U.S.A.' by Bruce Springsteen. Randy tightened the straps on his prosthetic leg and waltzed through the sliding doors and into the sunshine. Michael flamboyantly hopped out the truck in his tight American flag printed shorts with both hands on his hips, grabbed Randy's large duffle bag, then tossed it into the bed. After they entered the truck, Randy gave Michael a firm handshake and the truck drove off, Rand went into deep thought about all the things he'd been through including the loss of his mother. The same day he discharged his longtime friend and confidante Candyman had arrived hours later and, oddly enough, took Randy's old bed. Presumably it was Randy's due to the crash crew insignia etched on the wall behind the bunk. Candyman had both legs amputated and his days were numbered anxiously waiting for the right time to leave his life of misery and despair behind....

Chapter 10

The next morning Sarah was laying wide awake in bed unable to stop thinking about how her investigation of Randy Goldberg turned disastrous when the Hamden Police Department decided to take matters into their own hands by not following the F.B.I.'s strict orders. Ultimately, Hamden's hasty actions caused the entire investigation to culminate with not only numerous officers, lives lost but also it brought Sarah back to square one. Despite that, she got dressed then she decided to take a ride to New Haven to further survey the area of the first bombing.

Sarah drove down Dixwell avenue and stopped at the red-light intersecting Arch Street where she noticed an empty lot where the Catholic Church once stood. Sarah then pulled into the Burger King parking lot and, before exiting the vehicle, she grabbed her special eyewear, walked across the street, and placed them over her eyes. She pressed a button on one side of the frame and magically the historic church began to reappear. She walked around the perimeter of the church and visualized how immense and beautifully ornate the building once was on the corner. Sarah admired the detailed and abundantly colorful stained-glass windows in which many appeared as images of Angels whispering to Jesus. She stood behind the church for a few more minutes and tried to decipher the origin of art work.

Two hours later, Sarah was back at home about to embark on additional research of Randy Goldberg. She typed his name into the Google search bar and Randy's photo popped up with him in uniform. What she noticed next was the fact that he was labelled as being deceased with the cause of death – being an automobile accident. She began reading the associated article which stated Randy drove off the road and struck an oak tree. His black Toyota Land Cruiser caught fire leaving him trapped inside which, in turn, burned him and his vehicle to a crisp.

Sarah then dug further and stumbled upon his military history as part of the 3-33 Infantry Battalion AKA the crash crew. He specialized in bombs and his forte was handling and implementing all explosive materials. She scrolled down the list of soldiers who were affiliated with the crash crew and read aloud their names: Jason Welles AKA Candyman – deceased, Tony Thomas AKA Eagle eyes – deceased. There were also several other names all of whom were deceased except for the very last name – Platoon leader William Savage AKA Black cloud. Sarah quickly grabbed her i-Phone and texted Robert for some additional information on William Savage. She went back to the laptop and researched on article about military suicidal thoughts and how the army fought a continuing battle against suicide among the ranks. Military suicides began rising in the 2000's and, notably in 2012, claimed more soldier's lives than both the wars in Iraq and Afghanistan.

After revealing this new found information, Sarah backed away from her laptop and exclaimed, "Holy Cow!" She now knew something simply wasn't right so she felt the need for another criminal investigation into this matter starting first with the army, Sarah's i-Phone alerted her with a text from Robert stating, "there wasn't much info on Black Cloud. However, he was apprehended by military police in Wiesbaden, Germany more than five years ago for unknow classified reason. Sarah preceded her text with "thanks" then she continued with 'I am going to send you an article'. She wanted him to read it in hopes of seeing something she failed to recognize so they would have sufficient grounds for a federal investigation.

Sarah reopened her laptop and e-mailed the article to Robert. She was determined to learn more about Randy so she returned to his profile and noticed both that his mother died from cancer and, that he was an only child who never knew his biological father. For he abandoned them when Randy was just six months old. Randy was basically a good kid growing up and he was a straight A student in high school. Sarah also discovered another interesting fact about Randy when he discharged after a lengthy recuperation from the rehabilitation facility, he was picked up by Michael Walker who, at the time, owned a black Toyota Land Cruiser and whose sexual orientation was not only 'a typical' but he would also prey on soldiers with physical and Psychological impairment.

Sarah powered down the laptop, went upstairs, turned on the flat screen television, then proceeded to 'channel surf'. She stopped when she saw Shemar Moore chasing a criminal through a wooded area. So, she continued to watch 'Criminal Minds', put on some sweat pants, and made herself comfortable by laying across the bed. However, trying to ease her wary and cluttered mind was next to impossible because she was so preoccupied with Randy Goldberg. Sarah just needed him to make one costly mistake....

Chapter 11

Completely naked, Randy was sprawled across his bed sleeping with the television still on from the night before. Four lascivious scenes of 'Boot camp Fuckers #6' had been repetitively displayed on the screen since then. Unbeknownst to Randy, Sonny and Cher, his two French bulldogs, had not only accompanied him on the bed but they were also literally all over him for hours once he passed out. Truth is, if he would have realized they were so comfortably cozied up to him while he slept, he likely would have strangled both of them to death in the same manner as to Michael Walker who lewdly took advantage of him by stealing his manhood like a predatory Catholic Priest does to one of his altar boys. After a long day of relentless boozing together, Randy sawed off Michael's left leg then drove him down a desolate crushed gravel road in North Carolina. He then placed his lifeless body behind the steering wheel, strapped a large rock to the accelerator pedal slammed the vehicle into drive, and demolished it into a tree. The impact was so, severe it ignited the vehicle into a glowing gaseous fire! Randy then tossed his army dog tags into the burning truck and unapologetically walked away.

His bed sheets appeared as if they were thrown haphazardly across the floor and, above his nub, a fresh tattoo of a grenade with the words 'Run for your Life' inside it was now visible. His overturned drinking glass sat on the nightstand beside a seemingly empty bottle of Canadian Whiskey. While the ashtray was on the floor with cigarette butts scattered everywhere. Because the bed room door was shut, Randy's pack of camels was shredded to pieces by the bulldogs who also had managed to make his bedroom look like Hurricane Katrina swept through it. So, the dogs had nowhere else to run around and play. Cher was gnawing on the leather boot attached to his prosthetic leg leaving dozens of tooth marks. Sonny was toying with the sticky encrusted remote control on the floor forcing the channels to change every time he shook it.

Although still asleep, Randy began to slowly toss and turn, as if he was amidst, a bad dream. Unaware of his surroundings, he rocked from side to side. While the dogs watched a war movie on television. So, it seemed, based on the movement of Randy's body and corresponding shots fired and bombs dropped in the movie, those sounds were subconsciously manipulating his mind. Tanks were being fired and grenades were thrown and, with each blast, Randy's body movements coincided in unison. The dogs started to fight over the remote control and Sonny chomped on it hard enough to press the volume button which, in turn, raised it to the maximum at the same time a plane was being shot down. The explosion was so loud Randy suddenly jumped up, then fell onto the floor in an effort to 'take cover' as if he was caught in enemy crossfire. Both dogs scurried away from the loud noise and, when Randy finally came to his senses, he realized that he wasn't on the battlefield after all!

Bewildered and confused, Randy scanned the room as he wiped the sweat from his forehead then he screamed at both dogs, "I should had left you to die a long time ago with your owner!' In reality, however, he was simply lying to himself for he truly grew to cherish them. Besides, they surreptitiously were aware of all skeletons in his closet. Still fully exhausted, Randy wearily trudged over to the TV remote. While he surveyed the jumble of disorder that now existed in his bedroom.

No doubt, Randy was experiencing a serious hang over as his head throbbed in pain. He was barely able to scamper over to his nightstand then he opened a, draw to grab a bottle of prescription Xanax pills and twisted the top open. He then tossed a handful of pills into his mouth and, in the process dropped several on the floor. He grabbed the whiskey bottle in hopes there were a few drops of whiskey remaining to wash them down with but however, it was bone dry. So, he just chewed and swallowed them then he fought his way back onto the bed. Where he passed out again with Sonny hiding underneath the bed and Cher inside the close.

Chapter 12

Sarah was traveling en route to New York to meet with Robert for lunch at one of his favorite restaurants. So, they could further discuss the investigation. This pleasantly surprised her to discover Robert was in town for they had a longtime big brother – little sister relationship. Regardless of how wonderfully attractive she is, Robert always remained a consummate professional and would never cross the line. She showed up casually dressed in jeans and a cashmere sweater both of which accentuated her taut and toned mature figure. Her hair was braided into a long ponytail while her outfit was polished off with matching black leather Steve Madden booties.

The radio was set to a popular easy listening station playing an audiophile quality rendition of 'Man Eater' by Hall and Oates. Sarah was swerving randomly yet abruptly through traffic on I-95 and, judging by the stares of most passerby's, people traveling past her were complementing either her or her Mercedes Benz. So much so, they hadn't even noticed the gleaming New 'Individual' 7-series BMW one car ahead. Sarah glanced to her immediate left and saw a new pearl white Lexus GS450 Hybrid with the kids buckled in and their eyes glued to Finding Nemo on the television screen. As Sarah reached Stamford, traffic began to crawl at a snail's pace due to an accident nearly three miles away in which a party van collided with a school bus full of children en route to Six Flags

Amusement Park. After an hour delay, she finally proceeded onward past the scene and the rubber Necker's and, it appeared, by the grace of God no one was seriously injured.

As she approached New York City and the George Washington Bridge, she veered off onto FDR Drive via the Third Avenue Bridge then pressed a button on her steering wheel and spoke into her hands-free device to instruct her GPS to take her to the 'Hard Rock Café' 221 W. 57th St. (bet. Seventh Ave. and Broadway). As usual, the traffic was downright hectic in New York even utilizing the GPS and its quickest most direct route. Sarah entered a parking garage where an automated kiosk at the gate spewed out her receipt. She placed it inside her black leather bucket bag, put on the Gucci Sunglasses, and, while walking out of the garage, a Mexican man commented to another Mexican in Spanish "She is very beautiful".

Robert was standing out front of the Hard Rock Café. Keeping an eye out for Sarah who came walking over greeting him with a hug. She caught a whiff of his cologne which seemed to permeate the air before inquiring, "what are you wearing Robert?" He replied, "Tom Ford". Typically, she knows fragrances, however, this particular scent, she was not familiar with. Robert was dapperly attired as well wearing a structured sweater vest with a Ralph Lauren button-down shirt underneath, tailored dress slacks and, on his feet, were classic Wallibee Clarks. They made their entrance and requested a private area away from the crowd. But that was often next to impossible because the Hard Rock Café was an extremely sought-after establishment. Where tourists love to frequent due to the large collection of Rock and Roll Memorabilia. So, Robert and Sarah had to settle for the only available table as they chatted for a bit in anticipation of their meals.

A petite attractive brunette shod in a revealing form-fitting 'Hard Rock 'tee emerged with their food. Robert offered a smile to her as she bent over in front of him. While noticing the steam emanating from his baked potato. Completely famished from her journey into the Big Apple Sarah didn't waste any time dissecting her steak, into squares and devouring it. After the meal, they quietly began to talk about the article and the e-mail she sent to him. In fact, Robert was thoroughly surprised by the number of suicides and he expressed to her what really caught his attention was, '2012 had claimed more soldiers' lives than both the wars in Iraq and Afghanistan combined. Robert stated to Sarah, "he was going to contact his uncle who had deep-seeded ties within the military". Sarah exclaimed, "These issues clearly need to be addressed!" She then apprises Robert that Randy has been in disguise as an old man when out in public and, despite his prosthetic limb, he is entirely ambulatory. In fact, he moves around so well that, if people didn't know any better, they would think he was normal. Additionally, Sarah was convinced that Randy did not perish in a car accident as his death certificate cited for the burned body was actually that of Michael Walker, however, as certain as she was, she was not yet cognizant of the motive behind it. Regarding that mystery, Robert added, "the dental records will undoubtly rectify it!!"

The conversation between Robert and Sarah ultimately concluded when he stated that William Savage AKA Black Cloud who was currently incarcerated at a Fort Leavenworth, Kansas Facility serving a 20-year sentence for forging, then, issuing a multitude of bad checks using the identities of deceased military men. The prison warden claimed, 'he only had a few more months to live due to metastatic lung cancer that had now spread throughout his body'. Sarah shook her head in disbelief, Robert astutely changed the conversation by inquiring, "how long has it been since….?" Sarah quickly replied, "six years". Sarah's lover had passed away from injuries sustained from her motorcycle colliding with an oncoming vehicle. Before they parted ways, Robert offered Sarah a warm heartfelt embrace then she proceeded to the parking garage around the corner where she handed the Mexican parking attendant her ticket and a twenty-dollar bill. He then grabbed her keys off the peg board and handed them to her.

With a decidedly more profound sense of determination, Sarah fired up the Benz then pressed the same button on her steering wheel that voice activated her GPS navigation system by uttering, "I-95 North". She exited the garage while the GPS directed her to her destination and she cautiously headed home with 'start me up' by the Rolling Stones blaring on the radio. The traffic effortlessly flowed as she cruised down the highway and passed by some stellar-looking modern automobiles. One of which was a midnight blue Cadillac XT5 it must have been an exceptionally compliant and comfortable ride because the children were slumped against each other while peacefully sleeping in the backseat.

I'm still standing, a familiar Elton John tune, was playing on the radio. When Sarah approached the downtown New Haven exit a State Trooper had a white Chevrolet Malibu pulled over. The Trooper stood outside his cruiser and watched a young white lady who appeared to be inebriated trying to successfully complete a field sobriety test by walking a straight line. However, even with her arms out for balance, she continued to stumble and veer off line.

Sarah caught up to a silver Mercedes Benz C-Class Sudan with white leather interior. Operating it was a young black girl who appeared focused while holding the steering wheel tightly with both hands. Sarah glanced into her rear-view mirror and saw a platinum-colored BMW 7-series identical to the previous model creeping up from behind like a great white shark ready to pounce on an unsuspecting surfer, it literally flew past her and Sarah was so distracted that she did not even notice the red Ford pickup truck beside her with a pair of brindled bulldogs peering out the sliding back window.

Sarah finally arrived home, entered her garage and immediately texted Robert to let him know she reached home safely. Sarah exited the vehicle barefooted while carrying her shoes and, when she entered the house, she grabbed her book V is for vengeance and headed upstairs, she tossed her shoes to the floor, slipped into more comfortable attire, then laid across her plush bed with her book so she could finish reading the last chapter. Before passing out from exhaustion, she concluded her day by asking her amazon device, "what is the weather forecast tomorrow?" Alexa replied, "mostly cloudy with plenty of rain throughout the day".

Chapter 13

The continuous and delightfully soothing ambience of the heavy rain that inundated the area could be heard pelting the roof as Sonny and Cher laid patiently on each side of Randy in anticipation of his next move. Given the extremely unpleasant stench that emanated from the pair, it was increasingly difficult to decipher whether Randy or the dogs smelled worse – especially considering the lingering cigarette smoke.

Randy was positioned recumbently in his living room recliner holding a lit cigarette as he bellowed smoke into the stodgy air. While he stared at the cobweb – cornered walls riddled with quotes, he intently steadied his gaze onto one scribbled far away from the others which read, **Leadership is the ability to hide your panic from others**. Randy then pondered about that time in the rehabilitation facility when he found an army green cargo belt. He hid it for weeks, perhaps even months, before those pertinacious suicidal thoughts crept back into his mind and caused him to fasten it around his neck and pull with all his might until his muscles fortunately gave out. Eventually, he released his grip and, in turn, gasped for air. After two or three subsequent attempts, he discovered a more effective remedy to content with such suicidal ideation was to make others suffer.

Randy took a long drag from his cigarette, exhaled the smoke into the air, and started reading one of his newspapers whose headline caught his attention – 'House Explosion in Hamden CT'. He saw his old address 9 Windsor Rd. and twelve lives taken in the explosion. Randy's disfigured smile slowly appeared, he took another long drag from his cigarette and then he blew smoke circles out his mouth. After, he found out, the twelve dead were Police – officers. Randy said, "job well done". It's been years, since he last lived at that location. He was a strategist making it difficult for anyone who is after him. He knew they wasn't going to be ready for what he had in store, next time. Randy sluggishly got up from the recliner, after, he clipped a few articles from the heap of newspapers.

Randy slowly walked to the back door to let Sonny and Cher out. He opened the door looking at the rain pour down, both dogs would usually dash out but, this time they hesitated then walked out into the rain. Randy noticed a spider in the center of its web. It was spinning a web around a fly which had appeared to be trapped. He moved closer, capturing the spider by cuffing it with both hands. As he pulled away, the web broke, leaving the spider, crawling around inside his hands. After, a few moments of the tickling sensations, Randy placed his cuffed hands to his mouth. He then opened them, just enough for the spider to quickly exit, into his mouth. He used the right side of his mouth to chew the arachnid, and then he swallowed it.

The dogs had raced back inside the house, shaking the rain off of their drenched bodies. Randy shut the door, behind them and walked to the deep freezer. He opened it, a frozen runover possum with one eye still attached, stared him in his eyes. He easily moved the marsupial to the side, and underneath were several ziploc bags, next to a deer head. Each bag had the words 'deer meat' written across the front. He grabbed one of the bags and dropped it in the sink, leaving, the frozen meat to thaw. Sonny and Cher followed him back into the living room. He slouched in his recliner. Both dogs went back to their waiting positions on each side of the chair. As, if they were guard dogs, Randy lit a cigarette, then grabbed the tv remote changing the channel to animal planet.

Chapter 14

Sarah patiently stared at her laptop online playing chess against a little ole friend 12-year-old Abby Zugeroff from Russia. Sarah actually met Abby while in Russia shadowing Henry Dryer who went abroad in 2008 after he killed her partner. However, Henrys trail of terror was cut short, he met his fate in 2012. His case was officially closed with the word 'Deceased' stamped across his mugshot. Before, she flew back to the United States, Sarah and her K-9 CAP paid a visit to one of the most prestigious chess schools for kids.

Right then was where she met, Abby one of the students who had taken pictures with her and CAP. Sarah and Abby became very close, the kid was very challenging on the chess board. They would hookup twice a month to play a few games. The last time Sarah challenged her it ends in a stalemate. What Sarah couldn't quite figure out was Abby's premediated ability, she moved the pieces quick and had confidence behind it. Sarah would usually look over the board before she made a move.

Most people looked at chess as being the 'Game of Life', Sarah learnt to use the game as a mind exercising tool which keeps her focused, while out in the field searching for criminal minds. Sarah always felt the need to thoroughly investigate before she put her feet in their shoes. After all, she was one of the world's best profilers. Abby said, "Mate in one". Sarah slowly looked around the chess board. She noticed where Abby's queen was positioned so she surrendered by knocking over her king, then said, 'Good move". Abby replied, "the count is 3 to 1 my way". They both said, "good bye" and went offline.

Sarah stood up from the kitchen counter she placed her Stouffers cheese lasagna inside the microwave pressed 10 minutes, walked into the living room commanded Alexa to play 'I'll always love you' by Taylor Dayne blared from the amazon device. Seconds later, the microwave bell ring so she walked back in there took her meal out, and sat down at the counter to eat. While she ate her i-Phone began to play a tune. She answered, it was Robert. He sounds a little excited. He said, "those dog tags didn't match the body". Sarah replied, "was I right?" Before Robert answered he said, "the dental records also revealed whose body was inside the truck and indeed, it's Michael Walker. The autopsy showed his left leg was sawed off from the knee down!" Sarah end of the phone was silent. Robert asked, 'are you still there?' Sarah said, "I knew it Randy tried to fake his death". Her blood began to boil at the thought of this disordered bastard, out there roaming the city, and, at the same time leaving Sarah clueless to what his next move would be.

Robert could hear the anger in the tone of Sarah's voice, there was not much he could do or say except hope Randy get caught before he causes more destruction. Robert changed the conversation. He shared the information his uncle gave him, he said, the military Police were already involved. They had been investigating the Army for about 15 years now. They have an elite group who impersonate themselves as soldiers. Each month, they hand in numerous amounts of video almost all the footage shows mental abuse towards both male and female soldiers, and it's a lot more than standing in their face yelling and spitting!

The army had taken things a little too far, instead of soldiers being physically fit for war. They were broken down mentally struck with fear which caused many of them to go A.W.O.L. Some soldiers' minds were so shot they would rather get captured by the enemy who they knew would kill them, than to deal with their own superiors. And these are the men and women who are fighting for our country. Sarah was at a loss for words, she finally said, "This information explains a lot about the high suicide rate". Robert replied, I said the same thing to my uncle". Robert saw that he had to answer an important call that was coming in. So, he and Sarah said, "good bye" then hung up.

Sarah finished the rest of her lasagna, she turned on the laptop typed Randy Goldberg inside the search bar, moments later, his profile appeared. Sarah read certain articles about him; she knew most of it was fraudulent information. She continued to scroll through his page and wrote down small notes. The yellow paper had Mary L. Goldberg who is Randy's deceased mother and a large question mark for his father name. Michael Walker name was crossed out along with the handicap equipped van that Randy once drove. Sarah was patiently going over all the information she accumulated, leaving not one rock unturned.

Chapter 15

Today was a mournful day for the families and friends of the deceased, twelve police officers who lives were cut short in a deadly house explosion. The funeral was held at the largest church in Hamden, which roughly holds around three-thousand people. The Hamden chief of police and his family filled in the first three rows with the other victim families behind. The church was crammed, people stood against the walls. Due to the fact, many different law enforcement agencies had flown in to pay their respect, and the farthest happened to be from California. There were no physical remains to be placed in caskets, so, in remembrance of the twelve victims, large portraits from the youngest to the oldest took over the stage. Three of the victims were African American, two were Hispanic and the other seven were Caucasian, all in uniform.

A large screen showed video footage of each officers (life) from the beginning to the end, numerous, relatives stood and spoke of their experiences with the victims. A lot of Bible scriptures were read, there was not one person who didn't shed a tear. After the video footage was displayed of the three African American officers, all three of their mothers, broke down and had to be escorted, out the church for some air. It was definitely a sadden sight to have seen. Especially, for the deceased who have left small children behind that don't quite understand, what has happened yet and keep asking, "when is my daddy coming home?" The wives were seated together dressed in black with a net covering their faces, trying to compose themselves for the sake of the children. It was almost nearly impossible to do, knowing the transition from house wife to window had come so fast.

Sarah was seated in the very last row; she wore a black Atelier Versace pant suit with her black leather Marc Fisher heels. Robert Whirlwind was seated right beside her paying his respect. His whole attire was black on down to the shoes by Tom Ford. He held a gold inscribed leather-bound Bible. The Police 'chief' had finally broke down and had to be escorted out the church, after, he watched the footage of his baby boy wearing his Police officer hat. The chief remembered that day clearly, thinking back when he had a conversation with his son, he said, "one day you're going to be a Police officer". After, he was led out the doors, Sermon had gone on for hours, Sarah couldn't take it anymore. She saw five more wives get carried out the church, kicking and screaming, each one had a nervous breakdown.

Sarah tapped Robert on his knee to get his attention after, doing so, she stood up from her seat and he did the same, following her out the church door, placed sunglasses over their eyes to hide from the sun rays. While they walked to Robert's federally issued black Chevy Tahoe. Sarah recognized all the different news trucks and reporters, who waited patiently for the church doors to open. So, they could ask questions and get information about what went on inside the service. No, reporters were allowed inside the church, it was about respect for the colleagues and families of the victims.

Unknowing, Randy was seated in the middle row surrounded by law enforcement. He like to play with fire and mingle behind enemy lines. He sat quietly wearing all black as well, his top hat rested on his knee and sitting directly behind him. He heard a lady telling Tony and Tommy to sit still and be quiet. Everyone else just looked straight ahead at the Reverend standing behind the pulpit. Who spoke out loud, "the only sure thing in life is death? It will visit everyone and it is never a welcome guest?" The grieving filled church was silent. Until, the Reverend instructed, "open your bibles to Mark 5:35". Bible pages could be heard turning in search for the chapter and verse. Randy slowly scanned the crowd of people his hand shook while he placed a small device underneath his seat. He then stood, putting his hat on his head, grabbed his cane and slowly walked through the people towards the large doors.

Tony and Tommy had become impatient with sitting still and were now on the floor, counting people shoes. Tony grabbed the device from underneath the seat. He held it, inside his hand as if it was a 'Hot Wheels' car. The lady looked on the floor, she spoke softly, "Get off the floor and go use the bathroom". She figured maybe they need to use the rest room. Tommy ran off first, then Tony chased behind towards the bathroom. While the light on the device blinked every few seconds. Randy made it down the series of steps his suicidal thoughts kicked in and he let off a smirk. When he stopped in front of one of the news reporters, and said, "I had a blast in there". Tommy knocked the device out of Tony's hand while fighting over it, they watched if fall into the flushing toilet. Until, the device disappeared out of sight, they left out the bathroom running to their seat.

Randy sat inside his pickup truck, he reached into the glove compartment and grabbed a small black box with his hand. As he drove out the parking lot, he pressed a button with his finger, but nothing happened. He couldn't understand why the church didn't blow up! He looked through his rearview mirror as he drove further away waiting for an explosion. Tony and Tommy were quietly seated next to their mother. No one would ever know that their lives were saved.

Chapter 16

Sarah just finished showering after her morning job. She put on a white spaghetti strap tank top and some loose fitted pink sweat pants. She laid across her bed thinking about how inconsolable the funeral was yesterday. She flicked through the TV channels, stopped at News 8 'morning news'. Listening to the reporter talk about an underground explosion that took place yesterday in Hamden on Whitney avenue. It was unknown to what had caused a waterline to break and create a large water spout in the street. The news camera veered to the Hamden Fire Department and water work company, who were hard at work trying to control the overflow of water, which had caused a large area to be shut down.

Sarah didn't think much of it, but the church wasn't too far away. She left the bedroom and headed downstairs into the kitchen. She grabbed two protein power bars and sat at the kitchen counter. While she looked out the kitchen window, she thought about bringing Casper out for the first time. She already had a photo of Randy scanned along with his handicap equipped van. She had no idea the technology this drone truly possessed. Casper scan's everything in its path, sending high-definition quality images to the handheld device and it will alert you if the drone come in contact with the suspect.

She left the kitchen, walked into the living room and stopped in front of the large bookshelf. Where she finger scanned a row of hardcover books, she grabbed one which was a biography story. Titled: Twitch Upon a Star – The Bewitched Life and career of Elizabeth Montgomery by Herbie J Pilato. She turned the book around and read some of the details about Elizabeth Montgomery's life. And what caught Sarah's attention, Elizabeth was an advocate for aids suffers. She also supported all minorities including the Gay community, which was ironic because Sarah was a supporter of both. She held the book close to her chest as she scampered up the stairs.

An hour later, Sarah was more than halfway finished with the book. It most definitely had her full uninvited attention; the story went beyond the scenes of the bewitched star's career. Sarah read numerous exclusive interviews of Elizabeth Montgomery prior to her death in 1995. Sarah placed her book mark inside and closed the book, she slid it underneath her pillow for later on, tonight. She heard the neighbor kids in the backyard giggling, while she tied her New Balance sneakers. She walked to the bedroom window and seen the kids jumping up and down on a large circular trampoline. She smiled and left out the bedroom, heading downstairs. She passed through the kitchen and into the garage. She pressed the trunk button inserted on her vehicle key. The SL550 slowly opened, Sarah took Casper out the trunk. Casper stood in the palm of her hand; she mysteriously looked the drone over. She carried Casper and a hand-held tablet into the back yard. Sarah placed Casper on the ground while watching the kids do summersaults on the trampoline.

She turned on the device and the tablet showed a map of Connecticut. Once she tapped New Haven Casper quickly awoke and elevated into the sky. While going up, Casper began scanning the three kids as they bounced up and down, it calculated their height and weight. As well as, the black

Cadillac Escalade truck parked in the family driveway before disappearing into thin air. Casper was programmed to travel at 30 mph, it's 360° rotating lens had already scanned numerous people and vehicles, while it travelled south bound on I-91 towards New Haven. Sarah couldn't believe her eyes as she watched the screen on the table. She went and got inside the Benz, checked the glove compartment felt her Glock-9 which laid beside her F.B.I. badge. She drove out the garage en route to New Haven.

Casper was miles ahead passing through North Haven analyzing everything in its circumference. Moments later, Casper turned off the highway into New Haven after it found a complete match of the handicap equipped van. Its location was Chuck and Eddies junkyard, hidden deep in the yard, along with other rusted vehicles. Casper reported the match, immediately sending 190 Middletown Avenue to the handheld device which was the address. Casper navigated its way further into New Haven, while Sarah turned off the highway using exit 6, she made a right turn onto Middletown Avenue and proceeded towards Chuck and Eddies. She pulled up in front of the location, she saw a few people walking in the yard. So, she exited her vehicle walked inside the front entrance, showed her badge to the chubby white guy who sat behind the counter. He stood up, heart pounding and raised his hands in the air. While he stared at the letters F.B.I on her badge.

Chuck and Eddies had been raided numerous times in the past, they had a bad reputation for buying and selling stolen auto parts. Sarah instructed him to escort her out back into the yard. She said, "I am looking for an old model handicap van". She followed behind him and entered a graveyard full of vehicles. Almost, every vehicle had the word 'total' sprayed across them, which meant, no longer able to operate. Sarah looked around the muddy yard, she saw a pile of crushed vehicles, stacked on top of one another and the further they walked into the yard, weeds could be seen growing throughout, some of the vehicles. Sarah spotted the van which was stripped of everything. The only thing left was a rusted frame with weeds growing through it, indicating the van had been there for a long period of time. Sarah couldn't believe how Casper located the van, she left out the junkyard, turned around and said, "thanks for your service". The chubby white dude sat back in his chair, behind the counter, a sign of relief came over him. After thinking, he was about to get arrested. Sarah was a little pissed, she thought she was about to get some kind of break in her case. She pulled off, away from Chuck and Eddies, a cloud of dust lingered behind.

Casper was downtown on the New Haven green scanning every person, place and thing. Casper zoomed in on an old white guy laid on a bench who wore an old faded green army jacket with the stripes torn off. Moving along, Casper scanned a small group of people who stood in front of a black dude holding a backpack. Casper zoomed in on his hand, when it came out of the back pack. He held four packs of cigarettes, the drone scanned them, Newport (menthol) from the state of Delaware: illegal sales of Tobacco across state lines. Casper moved forward scanned a black male who sat four benches down playing 'three card Molly'. A crowd of people stood around him, a white kid pointed to the middle card. Casper scanned all three and recognized the card on the left is a different color from the other two. Casper continued along Chapel Street, scanned another black guy who stood at a bus stop dancing by himself, while people walked around him.

Sarah finally made it downtown, she was stopped at a red light at the intersection of Church Street and Chapel Street.

She watched the crowd stampede across the street in fear of the light quickly changing to green. She saw the New Haven green straight ahead and it looked like a lot of activity was going on. She caught another red light at the corner of Chapel Street and Temple Street. She watched two black guys who wore blue and yellow uniforms, they picked up trash at the corner. She figured the two gentlemen must work for the city of New Haven.

Casper was at Whalley Avenue and Sherman Avenue; people and vehicles were scanned as they left the gas station. Casper moved along scanning everything on Whalley and Ella Grasso Blvd. Sarah had become exhausted; her manhunt had turned into a needle in a haystack situation. She met Casper at the New Haven and Woodbridge Town line. After, she secured the drone inside her Benz truck, about to exit the Hess gas station, a red pickup truck drove, pass going into Woodbridge.

Chapter 17

After hours of roadkill hunting, Randy was parked in the driveway of his Woodbridge home. The 90° heatwave was a scorcher, he opened the truck door Sonny and Cher hurried out, a little irritated. Randy wiped his fore-head while he walked to the bed of his truck, a strong unpleasant odor took over. He grabbed four decomposed rodents by the tail, flies followed him as if they were fighting back for what was rightfully theirs. Randy swatted at the flies as he opened the gate to the backyard. The dogs ran to their usual location, disappearing in the grass. He then opened the back door and walked inside the house, shockingly without noticing there was a new spider web in the corner. He dropped the roadkill in the kitchen sink, before he turned to walk away, he saw something moving inside one of the rodents. So, he pressed down on the area and a substantial number of maggots squirted out, wriggling around in the sink. Randy eyes lit up with joy, he grabbed a handful, opened his mouth and let them drop inside. After, he swallowed them, he licked the sticky substance from the palm of his hand.

Randy unlocked the basement door, he walked down the dark corridor with his arms stretched out feeling for a string, he soon pulled it and a light bulb, flickered before it finally stayed on. He stood in a large room, it looked like a tool room. A place where he'd put together some of his most devastating explosives. There was a large map of the town of Woodbridge on the wall, and circled on it with a red marker was a convalescing home, it was actually several miles from his house. He walked to a calendar, it was the fourth of July, he couldn't wait for this day to come. He had promised himself to bring the elderly a 4th of July gift. He reached inside one of his steel cabinets, grabbed a metal marble sized ball with a hollowed inside and placed it on top of the table. He left the table and walked further into the basement, he returned, shortly after, with several different items dropping them on the table. He turned to his wall shelf, grabbed a blow torch and on his way back to the table, he pressed play on a dusty boom box.

Heavy metal music screamed out of the speakers, Randy's favorite song 'Russian Roulette' by Suffokate was playing, he screamed along singing, "let the boom spark a new world war, no will no way, I will not pay for a bastard's way, I am the anger that destroys this fucking place, no purpose for taken over I will end lives, your time is up I'm taken over, push till they break. You'll play the victim I play the pistol and paralyze your life". Randy held the blow torch as if it was an electric guitar, he grabbed the plastic face shield and secured it over his head to protect his eyes. He then marched to his operating table, where he began surgery.

One hour later, Randy had Sonny down there, he forced the metal ball down his throat, causing Sonny to swallow it. He then tied an American flag handkerchief around Sonny's neck. He carried Sonny upstairs, where the malodorous odor from the roadkill invaded his nostrils. He looked inside the sink at what he called the best protein in the world. He put Sonny down and grabbed a handful of maggots, dropped them into his mouth. He happily chewed and swallowed them, he figured Sonny and Cher were hungry. So, he put them to the test and placed a handful of maggots on the kitchen floor. Sonny and

Cher backed away, barking at the parasites. He grabbed Sonny fixed the handkerchief around his neck and carried him out the house.

Randy drove to the convalescing home, he pulled up to the entrance in his red pickup truck. He saw four senior citizens accompanied with aides, enjoying the beautiful 4th of July weather. He rolled down his window and waved for one of the aides, a skinny white lady wearing scrubs, approached the truck. He said, "I would like to donate my dog as a 'Independence Day' gift to the elderly." She looked and smiled at the cutie French bull dog, she couldn't refuse the offer. She reached in the truck and grabbed the dog, holding it in her arms, petting it. She said, "Thank you, may god bless your heart." She knew the dog was gonna bring joy into a lot of their lives. Especially, the lonely ones who families stopped coming to visit them.

Randy was on his way back home, he debated on which rodent he was going to devour first. He pulled into his driveway and exit the truck, reached in his pocket. He held a small black box in his hands, he looked up in the sky at the direction of the convalescing home. He then pressed a button and a big mushroom cloud of black smoke could be seen from afar.

Chapter 18

Sarah was on I-95 heading to Woodbridge, where an explosion had occurred, hours ago. She released Casper, before, she left the house. She knew the drone would make it to the crime scene much quicker. She had to fight her way through the busy highway traffic, she conversated with Robert through the stereo speakers. She said, "he struck again this time it was a facility." Robert was quiet for a moment...Then he said, "Randy has a nice place in Hell waiting for him". He felt the pain for all the lives that were just taken away. Sarah had no idea of the destruction Randy had caused yet, she didn't even know it was a convalescing home, he targeted.

Robert wanted to tell Sarah about what he'd just been through, catching his wife in bed with their son baseball coach. BUT he knew right now, wasn't a good time to mention it. Robert and his wife had numerous arguments in the past, he never thought things would lead to this. Casper was at the crime scene hoovering up above, scanning the massive black space and all the debris scattered, amongst the large slabs of concrete. Casper reported the exact location, sending the information to Sarah's tablet. She couldn't believe her eyes, when she saw the name of the facility which was The Sunshine Retirement Facility. She immediately said, "Robert, this son of a bitch blew up a convalescing home." Robert said, "Oh My God!!!"

Sarah drove into Woodbridge; she reached the demolished location. The news media stood along the cautioned tape area, recording footage, Woodbridge Police department and Fire department fought away the flames. She parked next to several Woodbridge Police cruisers, then she told Robert, "it's dooms day, and I will fill you in later with more details." She exits the vehicle, showed her F.B.I badge to the police officers and said, "I am a bomb specialist." The officers moved out her way, and watched as she approached the scene.

The fire was put out, but there were still a few hot spots, the fire fighters had under control. Sarah placed her eyeglasses over her eyes and pressed a button, the facility began to appear in sections until, every building was completed, she saw how large the place was…and quickly assumed there has to be at least two to three hundred fatalities. She walked closer towards the hologram facility and, noticed a green glow, which indicated the explosion happened on the third floor. She walked over to the Police officers and handed the chief one of her business cards, then said, "I would like a body count."

Sarah stood next to her Mercedes Benz, while she waited for Casper. The drone slowly landed on the vehicle hood, the Police offers all watched as Sarah took Casper and placed the drone inside the trunk. She got inside the vehicle and drove away from the scene, heading for the highway with the thought of putting a bullet in Randy's head on her mind. She finally made it home, she reversed into the driveway incase, she had to hurry out the house. She reached for her i-Phone and opened a text message; it was from Robert – I need to talk with you A.S.A.P. She figured after she get herself together, she would give him a call.

Chapter 19

NORFOLK, VIRGINIA

Robert was at home having a heated argument with his wife, Charlene. He had the bedroom door blocked so; she couldn't leave out the room. Luckily, Bobby their son spent the weekend with his grandparents. Robert begged Charlene not to divorce him, she could smell the booze on his breath. Charlene said, "I am sick and tired of spending all my nights alone, I have needs too!" Robert tried to justify himself by using his law enforcement job as his excuse. What he fell to realize, he was far from being Mr. innocent. He must've forgotten about all the bull crap, he put his wife through several years ago. Infidelity rumors, one was with Bobby's school teacher, another with Bobby's best friend mother, Angela who had become vulnerable after twenty years of marriage turned into divorce.

(The man forgives and forget; the woman forgives but never forget.)

And to this day, Charlene had to live with the fact of wondering if the son, Angela gave birth to was Robert's child. Robert had always denied the kid, even though they had similar facial features. Charlene held so much inside and she had always been a great wife to Robert. But everybody has a breaking point and Charlene's finally arrived. Robert was on his knees, he said, "I will change and spend more time at home." Unknowingly, he had already pushed his wife into the arms of another man and her mind was made up. She wanted out of her marriage to him, because her feelings were with Bobby's baseball coach, Matt. Robert's i-Phone had rung numerous times, he didn't answer, nor have he checked any of the text messages. He had roughly seventeen missed calls. Charlene yelled out, "Robert you're hurting me!" He held onto her arms pleading his forgiveness with a tight grip. He shook her, while the tears rolled down his face. Robert hadn't realized his own strength at this particular moment.

Charlene broke loose, she wore two bruised marks on her arms. She nervously backed away from Robert, fear kicked in, she screamed, "Robert do not touch me!" She realized how close; she was to the bedroom door. So, she quickly reached for the knob in a desperate attempt to open the door. Robert was quicker, he pushed it shut and snatched her away. He then said, "I will do anything to make it work!" Charlene heart wasn't with him, anymore, she started to cry then said, "I am pregnant with Matt's baby!" The look that came over Robert's face was pure evil his watery eyes were bloodshot red.

Charlene was seated on the floor in a corner, she held her knees with her head down. She couldn't face him no longer, she heard the sound of a gun cock back and when she looked up, he held a .45 caliber handgun, aimed at her head. Robert pulled the trigger, a hollow tip bullet, entered her forehead and exit out the back. Leaving, a large stain of blood and brain fragments on the wall, behind her.

Charlene's slumped body fell away from the wall, Robert came back to his senses from the loud shot! He grabbed, Charlene's lifeless body and held her in his arms. It registered; she wasn't coming back. So, he sat down beside her and placed the pistol inside his mouth, then pulled the trigger, leaving the same stain on the wall as she had.

Chapter 20

Randy laid back in his lazy boy recliner after a good day of work. If he could pat himself on the back, it would be for a job well done. He unstrapped his prosthetic leg it fell to the floor, which indicated he was extremely comfortable. He was stuffed after eaten a full course meal, his favorite 'roadkill.' He poured himself, a double shot of whiskey. He slammed the glass on the table, flicked through the TV channels, stopped at News 8. He saw a news reporter doing a story about the bombing, which took place earlier in Woodbridge.

Randy unbuttoned his shirt, patted his bloated belly and released some gas, the unpleasant smell filled the air. He watched the news footage, the scene showed burning debris, where the convalescing home once stood. He stared into the pretty news reporter eyes, as if they were face to face and he appeared to be the dominate one. He quietly said, "assume the position." In Randy mind, he had become the drill sergeant from boot camp fuckers, he gave a direct order to the reporter. He tossed back, another double shot of whiskey without taking his eyes off his prey.

The news reporter said, "The body count was at 286 and people were still uncounted for and it would take a few more days of searching and contacting relatives. Before, a final count could be determined. Randy glanced to the side of his chair and saw Cher wasn't by his side. She was over in the corner curled up as if, trying to stay far away from him. The female news reporter disappeared from the screen, Randy lit a cigarette and watched the weather man who said, "tomorrows forecast it's going to be lots of sunshine." Randy looked at the ceiling where a quote was written, he read, **"The quietest place to be found, rest inside a Peaceful soul."** He then tossed back another double shot of whiskey and seconds later, the room began to spin causing him to pass out.

Chapter 21

Sadly, Sarah had received the news about Robert later that night it explained why he never got back in touch with her. She couldn't believe what she had heard, Sarah plate was already full with this sick in the head bastard, on the loose, running around bombing places, killing innocent people. And, to now find out her best friend, who she knew for several years killed his wife, then himself. It was a lot for her to swallow, the thought came across her mind…. was he trying to tell me something in our last conversation? And if so, why didn't he? Then she thought about missing his phone call and not responding right back.

All that matter right now, she had to book a flight so she could pay her respect to him. Sarah made phone calls, she searched for the next flight to Virginia. She called her father, Peter who was the only man that could comfort her in such a saddened time. Sarah was Peters only child, daddy's little girl, he immediately told her to come home for a week or two. So, she could take a break, Peter knew she worked hard. When it came down to her job and for her to come home, it would be a great stress reliever.

The next day Sarah was dressed early, she wore a loose fitted black and white Adidas track suit. She walked over to the large bookshelf in search for a nice, long, book to read. She looked out the window before, she grabbed Private by James Patterson and M. Paetro. She turned the book over and read the blurb – former marine helicopter pilot Jack Morgan runs Private, the world's most powerful investigative firm. Sarah smiled and placed it inside her backpack. She watched a silver Mazda CX-9 pull up; she saw the uber stick in the front windshield. So, she grabbed the backpack tossed it over her shoulder, set the house alarm and walked out the front door. She was greeted by an older white lady who sat behind the steering wheel with a smile. When she entered the back of the vehicle. The uber driver program Bradley International Airport into the GPS, and then the vehicle drove off.

Sarah looked around and saw how clean the vehicle was.... The uber driver sparked a short conversation, when she asked what do you thing about this psycho who's running around bombing everything? Sarah responded, he's a maniac who has to be stop! The uber driver said, "he'll make a mistake sooner or later". The conversation switched to President Trump, she asked do you think he will get voted for a second term? Sarah gave her honest opinion and said, "I don't think so but anything is possible." They both remained quiet for a few minutes, Sarah starred out the window at vehicles as they passed by...

The uber driver made it to the airport, she waited patiently in the long line of vehicles to the entrance. The driver finally reached the front entrance, Sarah exits the vehicle with her backpack on her shoulder. She entered into the crowded airport, thanking God, she paid for her ticket online last night. She looked at the large board and saw her flight wasn't until another thirty minutes. So, she went and brought an apple Danish then made her way towards a line. Where people put their luggage and carry-on bags through a large X-ray machine. Sarah walked into the metal detector, and noticed off to her right, two security guards had a female with her hands in the air. One of the guards moved a wane around her body. Sarah went through without any problems. She always knew to travel light, especially at the airport.

Sarah got aboard and moments later, people started to crowd onto the plane. The aisle was crammed while luggage was being placed up above inside the storage area. The captain voice came over the intercom. He said, "the plane will be ready for take-off in five minutes, and everyone should stay seated until in the air." Sarah saw a pregnant lady being buckled in by her spouse. Sarah had a window seat. She watched the plane catch speed before it flew off into the sky. Once in the air…. The captain came back on the intercom, he said, "the flight attendants will come around shortly for those in need, and everyone enjoy the flight". A few minutes later, two stewardesses walked down the aisle and offered peanuts, small bottled waters to each passenger. Everyone looked comfortable in the air, the Tv schedule had some pretty good movies on it. Sarah pulled out her book and every now and then, she would stop reading to gaze out the window at the clouds in the sky. She thought about what the uber driver said, "he'll make a mistake sooner or later." Sarah eyes became heavy when she got to chapter fourteen. So, she decided to take a quick nap.

Twenty minutes later, Sarah was awakened by the pregnant lady scream, my water just broke!!! Her husband nervously held her hand. She grabbed her stomach and told him to do something but, he was lost for words. She had begun to take deep breaths, a stewardess frantically stood in front of the couple, she looked around then asked is there a doctor on board? We have a passenger who's in labor. Just as Sarah stood to walk over a petite white woman stated I AM! Then said, "Dr. Karen Walls is my name." She rushed over with a small plastic medical bag, placed gloves onto her hands, Sarah held a damp rag on the pregnant lady's forehead, someone yelled out we have another doctor on board! She rushed over towards Sarah and Karen with a handful of towels. She too wore latex gloves; Karen hands were underneath the pregnant lady's sundress. While the second doctor instructed breath and push, the pregnant lady gasp for air, squeezed her husband hand and pushed. Karen said, "here come the head." Sarah said, "push, push, Push!!!" After, five more pushes a baby boy was born someone asked the husband, "do you have a name?" He starred at his son while Karen wrapped him inside a towel, placed him into his mother arms. The husband softly said, "Skyler". His wife just smiled as she cradled their new born. The rest of the flight almost all the passengers catered to the new mother who was blessed after delivering a healthy baby boy while being thousands of miles up in the sky.

Three hours later, the airplane made a quiet landing in Virginia the captain could be heard once again, he said, "ladies and gentlemen we are now in Virginia." All the passengers let the new family exit the plane, first. They all walked through the terminal, made it out of the airport, vehicles were lined up and uber drivers held signs in the air with people names scribed on them. Sarah walked down the long line of parked vehicles until, she finally saw her father who hadn't aged a bit with his trimmed cut beard, Cartier wood framed eyeglasses, standing next to his 82 Rolls Royce Silver Spur. Peter had the biggest smile on his face as, Sarah ran into his arms after, the long embrace, she complemented him on his vehicle. Because the last time she seen it, the vehicle had a lot of work to be done, including a paint job. And now the Rolls Royce looked as good as new, it gleamed with the Jade green paint job. Peter opened the door for her, she handed him the back pack then, she sat inside on the butter soft leather interior and stared at the wood grain dash board and door panels. Peter tossed her back pack into the back seat, as he got in the driver seat. A few passer byes complemented the Rolls Royce, Sarah smiled and looked at her father, she then said, "thanks." Peter drove off, leaving out of the airport.

Sarah started to tell her father about the most amazing thing that happened on her plane ride. She said, "A lady gave birth while on the plane." Peter replied, "really." Then he said, "it's going to be a special moment for the couple, one they will never forget." Sarah smiled after listening to what her father just said. Peter drove Sarah to his house, where they caught up with a little father and daughter time. She noticed that her father was still single, because there were no signs of another woman anywhere. After, Sarah mother divorced Peter, she re-married a much younger man, a year later. Sarah always believed the reason for their divorce was a stupid one. All because her dad spent more time in the backyard, where he would fix old cars, which was a longtime hobby of his. Sarah mother use to always claim, he loved them cars, more than her. Sarah still couldn't see no wrong in her father eyes. Peter was right by her side, when she went through the tragedy of losing her girlfriend. Peter even surprised her and paid for Selena's head stone.

Peter raised from his lazy boy chair and said, "let's take a walk into the backyard." Peter showed Sarah his classic car collection, she saw six vehicles covered underneath leather covers. He pointed out each car. First, a 1957 Porsche Speedster, Second, a 1960 Mercedes Benz 190 SL, third a 1960 Chevrolet Corvette Convertible, fourth a 1969 Maserati Ghibli, fifth a 1991 Ferrari Testarossa. He then said, "the sixth one is my favorite, this bad boy is the reason why your mother filed for divorce." He removed the black leather cover and introduced Sarah to a beautiful Jaguar XK140MC Roadster. The sunshine gave the silver paint job an extra sparkle. In Sarah eyes it was just an old vehicle, but in, Peter eyes it's a prized possession. Sarah looked at the new burgundy leather interior as, she walked around the vehicle. Then she asked, "what is that over there?" Peter looked and said, my new project a 1985 Land Rover Defender 90." Sarah stared at the rusty truck with numerous missing parts.

Peter glanced at his Rolex Submariner; he knew Sarah was probably going to visit Selena's grave site tomorrow. So, he said, "I better get you home." She looked at her watch then said, "yes." Peter went and grabbed his car keys off, the living room table and they left out the house. He held open the car door for her, and walked around to the driver side. He started the vehicle and asked, "when is your friend funeral?" Sarah said, "it's in three days around 10:00 am." Peter drove off thinking to himself, what suit to wear when he attends his daughter's friend funeral.

Chapter 22

Sarah woken the next morning and for some strange reason, all she could remember was a weird dream. She was the owner of an antique car dealership. She sat up in the bed, looked at her night stand and grabbed her gold picture frame. It was a picture of her and Selena standing in the water, taking a selfie together at Virginia Beach. She placed the frame back onto the night stand, then she got out the bed, unfastened her bra, leaving it behind. She walked into the bathroom to urinate and while she sat on the toilet, out of nowhere Randy came into her mind. She wondered, what his next move was going to be. She flushed the toilet, stepped out of her panties.

Sarah looked at her flawless body in the mirror, she untied her top knot, letting the hair loose. She turned on the shower, waited for it to steam, her bathroom mirror quickly became misty. She stepped into the shower; water sprayed onto her body. She reached for her loofa and dove body wash. She started washing herself, rinsing the soap suds off her body. The hot water had her in a relaxed mode, while running down through her hair. She reached back into the shower head rack, grabbed a purple device, she twisted the top off and pressed a button, the device started to vibrate.

As the hot water rolled down the water proof device, she placed it down in-between her legs. Sarah made a jerk movement as if she was a virgin about to get penetrated for the first time. She slowly worked the device near her clitoris, where it buzzed in a circular motion, causing her to take light breaths. Sarah clitoris quickly came out from its hiding place. She touched it with her finger, making a love connection. Sarah was hot and horny and there wasn't no stopping now, she began having intercourse with the device. She started to moan and loss control, she found herself on the shower floor. Her legs wide open giving the device all she had. The shower water chased her love juices down the drain.

Sarah was hungry for more; she licked the device a few times before squatting up and down on it. She laid in the shower sideways, taking the device from another angle. It felt like she was making love in the pouring down rain. She had become a sex slave to the device. She had orgasm after orgasm. The device was turned up to its highest level, all Sarah could do at this point was scream! She slowly became light headed as if she was about to faint, but the device wouldn't let her. It had full control over her, until, she finally fought her way out of the shower. She made it to her bed, where she laid their soak and wet holding the picture of her and Selena close.

An hour later, Sarah woke up laying on the picture, she quickly grabbed it from underneath her and scanned it, making sure the glass didn't crack. She gave Selena a kiss, then placed the picture back on top of the nightstand. She got out of the bed, feeling like a new woman. She was way over do; it was only right for her to release some tension.

Sarah got dressed for the day, she wore one of Salena's Rolling Stones t-shirt and some blue jeans. She went downstairs into the kitchen, ate two bowls of Honey nut Cheerios. She walked into the living room, turned on the television, sat on her couch and reached for her i-Phone. She called, the Quantico F.B.I facility, and spoke to her supervisor, F.B.I. Agent Douglas

Turner, he was the agent who interrupted her profiler class. Sarah asked, "could you have someone substitute my profiler class a little longer?" Douglas said, "sure no problem". Then she said, it's going to take longer than I thought, trying to apprehend this suicidal bomber. She realized she wasn't up against no amateur; Randy Goldberg was the real deal and he meant business. They changed the conversation to Robert Whirlwind, Douglas said, "it was a sad situation." Sarah replied, "it was." Minutes into the conversation, Douglas had to take an important call so, they hung up.

Sarah grabbed the bike keys off her key rack, walked in the back of the house, pulled the black cover off, her 2012 Suzuki GSX R1000. She put on the helmet and got onto the bike, turned it on, the bike began to roar like a lion in the jungle. She pulled off heading down the road. She stopped at a florist shop to get some roses, before she got onto the freeway.

Twenty minutes later, Sarah rode into a cemetery, she parked the motorcycle and walked down a row of tomb stones. She stopped in front of a beautiful head stone; a picture of Selena was inserted into the stone. It had angels carved on both sides and a gold plaque: **Gone but never forgotten... forever in our hearts.** Sarah placed the dozens of roses inside a metal flower vase, then she sat down on the freshly cut grass, next to Selena's headstone.

Sarah started to reminisce about the time, her and Selena wore matching rainbow-colored LGBTQ tee shirts. They entered the karaoke contest and won, it.

Singing their favorite song, True Colors by Cyndi Lauper. Everyone waved their hands, back and forth, while they sang the song. A tear rolled down Sarah's face, she said, "I miss you." She got really emotional, while she explained how difficult life was without her. She began to laugh, when she told Selena that her father finally finished that old rusty Rolls Royce. He had in his backyard and it turned out to be a beautiful car. Sarah looked up at the sky and said, "you would have loved to ride in it." Then she said, "Robert was gone, he took his own life, after he taken Charlene's and his funeral is tomorrow." She stood up and said, "you will always have the key to my heart." She bent down and gave the picture of Salena a kiss, before she left the grave site. Sarah put the helmet over her head, started the motorcycle and rode out of the cemetery. She let the bike roar, while she headed to the freeway. She rode around for a while; she took a route that her and Selena use to always ride together.

Chapter 23

5am the alarm clock alerted, Sarah woke reached over and stopped the clock, she laid in bed a few extra minutes. She got out the bed put on some sweats, then dashed downstairs into the kitchen. She made herself a hot cup of joe before she left out the house. She started to jog down the street, it was little foggy, cool and the smell of morning dew set the pace. While she inhaled and exhaled the air, six houses down the street, she saw three deer's inside someone's front yard. Licking, the water out of a large round cement center piece. Usually, birds would take baths inside there, soon as Sarah approached the house, all three deer looked at her and sprinted towards the backyard, disappearing in the woods. She kept jogging and turned onto another street, the sight of her seeing deer was nothing new. There was a lot of wooded areas, where she lived in Virginia. She was on her forth lap around the block, she noticed a dead snake lying flat in the road, she returned home after six laps.

Sarah undressed and walked into the bathroom to shower, she had a long day ahead of her. Twenty minutes later, she was laying out her outfit for the funeral. A Black Christian Dior dress and a pair of Nine-west black leather open-toe heels. She got dressed, looked at the mirror, admiring her natural beauty, she twirled around a couple of times before she grabbed her black clutch purse. She went into the kitchen, ate a fruit salad, she looked out the kitchen window and saw a deer walking along the edge of some trees. Her i-Phone rung it was her dad, he said, "I am outside." Sarah replied, "ok." She went looking out the living room window and smiled.

Her dad was dressed to impress wearing a black Armani suit as he stood next to his silver Jaguar Roadster. Sarah left out the house, she looked stunning as she walked to the vehicle. She gave her dad a warm embrace, catching a whiff of his cologne. She recognized the scent to be Armani Code, she complimented him on his attire. He held the car door open and said, "you don't look so bad yourself." Sarah smiled while getting inside the car, she enjoyed the comfort of the soft burgundy leather seat. Peter got back inside then drove off heading to the freeway.

Chapter 24

A rain shower passed by, Peter drove into Norfolk, Virginia the sun had come out. Sarah asked, dad do you know where the church is? He said, "yes an old buddy of his funeral was there." As he drove into the city area of Norfolk, he saw a crowd of uniformed officers. He pointed to the church and said, it's right over there." Peter drove in the large parking lot, him and Sarah exit the vintage Jaguar. She shook a few hands and introduced her dad. All her colleagues were dressed in uniform.

Sarah and her dad found a seat in the middle row, she glanced at the closed casket. She saw a large portrait of Robert in uniform, Supervisor Douglas was seated directly in front of her, she tapped him on the shoulder. Douglas turned around and Sarah introduced him to her dad, they shook hands. Douglas told Sarah the sad news, "Charlene's family don't want her, buried beside Robert." Sarah replied, "I heard they wouldn't let Bobby attend his dad's funeral." They both went silent, Peter said, "it's a sad situation." Robert received a lot of love; some powerful people came out to pay their respects. The scale for suicide amongst law enforcement officers was high, do to these very same reasons.

An organ played in the background; the Reverend waited a few more minutes for everyone to be seated. He stood behind the pulpit and adjusted the microphone. The organ stopped playing and then the Reverend said," we are all gathered here today. In this house of God to pay our respects to a great man. A beloved father of one and not to mention a husband. He also was a law enforcement officer who took pride in his job."

The Reverend read several different verses from his bible, there were two that stuck out...

> For the wages of sin is death: but the gift of God is eternal life through Jesus Christ our lord.

> Romans 6:23

> And God shall wipe away all tears from their eyes: and there shall be no more death, neither shall there be any more pain: for the former things are passed away.

> Revelation 21:4

An usher handed the Reverent a white cloth so, he could wipe the sweat from his forehead. He sat down and the organ began to play again. One at a time, each row ascended and moved forward to touch the casket. Robert's mother wouldn't leave from in front of her son casket, she was down on both knees crying. Robert Senior had to remove her from the casket so other family members and close friends could share a private word or two. Sarah and her dad walked up to the casket, she leaned over and gave the casket a kiss, then walked away and said, "Now you're in a better place."

Everyone left the church, following behind the black hearse to the cemetery. Relatives stood around and watched the casket as it was lowered six feet below. Everyone tossed flowers inside the grave. Sarah feet began to throb, because of her, high heel shoes. She never wore them for such a long period of time. People started to clear out, only family members stayed behind.

Sarah and her dad walked to his vehicle, they had a quick conversation about getting something to eat, before her 4:30 pm flight back to Connecticut. As Peter was about to drive out the cemetery entrance, he was suddenly pulled over by a black jeep wrangler with tinted windows. A tall well-built man with a receding hairline, jump out demanding to speak with Sarah. He introduced himself as Cody Broder the Head of operations, he looked at Peter then said, "I am sorry if I startled anyone." Sarah patted her dad on the shoulder then she said, "he'll be alright." Cody explained himself as being a close friend to Robert's family. Sarah asked, "does this have anything to do with what's been going on in the military?" Cody said, "Absolutely." He told Sarah, "there is high ranking and retired military officials, being apprehended right now as we speak, brought up on murder and conspiracy charges, thanks to Robert and the information you shared with him." Sarah was excited to hear the good news; Cody handed her a card before getting back inside his Jeep. Peter drove out of the cemetery and Sarah explained to him what was going on, while on their way to one of his favorite Steak Houses, outside of Richmond.

An hour later, Pete was inside the airport with Sarah, he waited for her flight to be called and minutes later, a voice spoke over the intercom, all passengers can start boarding Jet Blue through terminal one headed to Connecticut. Peter embraced Sarah and kissed her on the forehead. He let her go then said, "have a safe flight and call me." He stood there and watched Sarah walk through the terminal. She turned around one las time and waved bye to her dad.

Chapter 25

Back in Connecticut, Sarah profusely worked on her case, she almost forgot to text her dad so he could know she make it back safely. She had watched numerous video footage Casper accumulated; her days felt awkward especially now that Robert was no longer present. She became a little emotional, a tear rolled down her cheek, she knew her and Robert would have already discussed the military indictments. She respected the fact that Cody made all of this happen on the day of Roberts funeral, it was in memory of him. The thought of it brought a smile to her face.

Sarah reached out to different companies that sold prosthetic parts, she asked each distributor if they had Randy Goldberg in their system. Each company responded back, no one by that name is registered in our data base. Once again, Sarah was brought back to square one, and to make matters worse, she just found out the death toll, reached 396 in the convalescing home bombing. She felt for all the victims and their loved ones. She requested all street cameras coming and going from the Sunshine Retirement Facility. When she received the footage and tried to watch it, the indistinctness of the footage was terrible.

Sarah typed in military indictments, she used google, a big article appeared on the bright screen, **Headlined: one of the militaries biggest bust ever**. Underneath, Sarah begins reading the article, which stated, people were being charged with murder and conspiracy, it showed 21 names and photographs.

She scrolled down looking at the men mug shots, she couldn't believe her eyes, at how frail most of the men looked, quite a few were retired. When 12 of the ex-military men houses were raided, they fell out and had heart attacks, died on the spot. The article was getting more and more interesting.

Sarah stood up and walked away from the laptop, she went into the refrigerator grabbed her turkey and cheese foot-long sub and a bottle of Polar Spring water. She sat back down in front of the laptop and took a bite from her sub. Suddenly, out of nowhere, she heard the neighbor screaming in their backyard. Her husband Jeff came running out the house, he had a Louisville slugger in hand. Mandy pointed to the swimming pool, he dropped the baseball bat, climbed up the ladder and jumped into the pool. He dragged his youngest daughter Miley out, by this time Sarah had ran over to help, she gave Miley mouth to mouth, pressed down on her little chest, pinched her nose then repeated the same method. By the grace of God, Miley started to cough and spit water out her mouth.

Mandy fell to her knees and held Miley in her arms. Jeff was soak and wet, he grabbed his baseball bat. Started swinging at the pool. Water was everywhere in the backyard.

Mandy couldn't thank Sarah enough for saving her little girl life. Sarah gave young Miley a hug and then said, "you're going to be alright." Mandy took Miley inside the house and Sarah walked back into her house. Sarah took a look out the kitchen window, she saw Jeff destroying the pool. He finally threw the bat down.

Sarah lost her appetite, she put the rest of her foot-long sub back in the refrigerator. She shut down the laptop, grabbed her bottle of water and went upstairs. She laid across the bed, reached for her book I-Private. So, she could finish reading the last two chapters.

Chapter 26

Randy was looking at himself in the bathroom mirror, he stood there silently for a moment. Then he screams out loud, "I Am reporting for duty Sir!" He had his hand raised high in a salute position and behind him in the mirror his platoon was present. Randy looked like a psycho path with nothing more than death in his eyes. Everyone in his mind disappeared from the mirror.

Sweet dreams by eurhythmic could be heard blaring somewhere in the house. Randy touched the permanent scar that rest on his disfigured face. He opened his mouth and most of his teeth were gone or rotted. He went inside the medicine cabinet; different expired bottles of psyche medications were there. He grabbed a straight razor, then closed the cabinet door. He turned on the sink facet, rinsed the blade through the cold water. He then, placed the sharp blade to his face, and removed all the growing particles of hair.

Randy rubbed some kind of sticky clear substance on his face. He grabbed some sort of hair piece, it looked mostly gray with white specks throughout. He neatly placed it around his chin and up to where his sideburns would start. He then looked at each side of his face, making sure he had the perfect fit. Randy had disappeared underneath his disguise, transforming himself into an old man. He took his dentures out of a small cup of water and placed them inside his mouth. Instantly, giving him a full set of cigarette-stained teeth. He slowly placed the last piece of disguise onto his head, which was an old Boston Rd Sox cap. He smiled at himself, then he said, "Mr. Leroy Peterson." He admired his new identity.

Mr. Leroy Peterson picked up a white plastic sprint bag, inside were six activated I-Phones. The whole house was filthy and the unpleasant smell was unbearable, dead flowers were in a vase on the kitchen window ledge. The home had no more life to it, Cher had droppings on the living room carpet. Leroy walked into the living room, Cher ran underneath the couch, she saw Randy as a stranger, when he was in disguise. Leroy left out the back door, he carried the plastic bag. He got inside the pickup truck, placed the bag on the passenger seat. He drove out the driveway, heading to the highway, on his way to Bridgeport.

Leroy was on the highway, he looked to his left and found himself, side by side with a Chrysler 300. It cruised right on by him; he lit a cigarette while driving across the Housatonic River bridge. There were huge bill boards on both side of the highway. One read – IF you see something, say something. The other read – Do not touch anything you find, report it to the police. Leroy looked through his rearview mirror, he saw an Audi Q5 Quattro speed up, the SUV zoomed by blowing the horn at him. While it switched lanes, Leroy called the driver, an idiot! He watched the SUV as it impelled in front of him.

Leroy recognized the New York license plate; A Mercedes Benz E-320 wagon was about to switch lanes. When the Audi SUV crashed into the Mercedes Benz, causing it to hit a Mitsubishi eclipse, flipping the small vehicle onto its side. Sliding down the highway in a trail of sparks, until, it crashed into the guardrails, coming to a firing stop! Vehicles swerved out the way, to avoid the accident. Leroy drove around all the vehicles, he laughed, as he passed the smashed Audi. The driver laid on the side of the road, he must had been thrown out the SUV from the impact.

Leroy drove off the Bridgeport exit, he saw another one of those bill boards, they happened to be everywhere. He drove down main street, turned on his stereo. Tell it to my heart by Taylor Dayne was on, he turned the knob, changed the radio station. Mr. Telephone man by New edition blared through the speakers, he quickly changed it again. Into the night by Phil Collins played so, he left it there. Now, he looked for areas where he could place the iPhone. He noticed how small downtown Bridgeport was. He stopped in front of the Holiday Inn, opened his passenger door, leaned over and dropped a iPhone onto the sidewalk. He drove further down main street and left a iPhone, behind at the bus stop.

He parked the pickup truck, then he exits the vehicle and walked down golden Hill Street. Where he left a iPhone near the court house, he dropped another one at 300 Congress Street, right in front of the Bridgeport Police Department. He went back to the truck, and drove to Seaside Park. The weather was nice, the park had clean cut grass, a beautiful view of the water. He strolled through the park and left two iPhones in different areas. A black girl went walking by pushing a baby stroller, Leroy smiled at the baby. As she passed by him, heading in the direction where he left a iPhone in plain view. She turned around and looked at Leroy as he kept walking, she said, "God, that old man stink." Leroy looked around then he said, "this is going to be interesting." He made it to his vehicle, lit a cigarette and drove out the park, listening to – eyes without a face by Billy Idol.

On Main Street, a white dude snatched the iPhone off the ground and hurried into the Holiday Inn. Further down, Main Street, a Spanish girl stood alone at the bus stop, she found the iPhone and placed it inside her backpack. Another, iPhone was retrieved by a Police Officer; he brought the phone inside the Police Department. He asked, "did anyone lose a cell-phone?" No one responded, so, he left it with a female officer who worked the lost and found department. The last two iPhones were discovered by two black girls at Seaside Park.

Leroy looked at his Timex watch, the time was 4:15 PM, he was driving down the highway headed home. He drove pass the accident scene, and saw the vehicles being placed onto separate flatbed trucks. The smashed-up Audi and badly damaged Mitsubishi eclipse caught his attention. Leroy drove by with a smirk on his face...hoping the driver of the Audi SUV didn't make it.

Meanwhile, the six individuals who received a present from Leroy, had no idea they became suicide bombers. The white dude was inside his hotel room, on the tenth floor, laid across the bed watching Porn-hub on the iPhone. The Spanish girl was seated on the crowded city bus next to a pregnant lady, she was making her an Instagram account. A black dude was talking to his public defender in the hallway of the court house. He had the iPhone in his pocket, while trying to get another court date, because today was his sentencing day. The female Police officer was stuck at her desk on the iPhone, playing candy crush. The two black girls at Seaside Park, one attended a family cookout, she took selfies with her daughter and the other black girl had left the park. She sat inside her friend car, making a face book account, while she waited for her to come out, the day care with her children. Miles away, Leroy passed through Milford, he reached inside his glove compartment. He grabbed a small black box and pressed the button with his finger. Six areas in Bridgeport exploded bringing down buildings and leaving other places badly destroyed.

Chapter 27

Sarah released Casper into the air, after she received the disturbing phone call about what just took place in Bridgeport, the Police Department and court house explosion. Casper was headed to Bridgeport, scanning everything along the way. Sarah received another phone call; she was told there had been four more explosions in Bridgeport. She rushed up the stairs and into her bedroom, turned on the television. So, she can see what in the hell was going on…

News 8 was covering the Police Department explosion and the court house as well. Sarah pressed the TV remote changed the channel to Fox 61, they were covering the Holiday Inn explosion with an extended news team, covering the Main Street and North Avenue explosion. NBC News reported the explosion on Park Avenue, it happened right in front of the ABCD Daycare. CBS News showed live footage at Seaside Park, where there had also been an explosion. Vehicles were scanned left and right on I-95, Sarah quickly got dressed, while watching the Fox 61 News coverage. Witnesses talked about how they saw the city bus pick up passengers, and on its way to the next bus stop, blew up! An older black lady stepped in front of the news camera, she said, "This had to be a suicide bombing." Sarah tied her sneakers while listening to people talk about what they witnessed.

Sarah left out getting into her vehicle, she sat inside the Benz, looking at the tablet. She watched Casper scan what was left of the Holiday Inn. She noticed a multiple lens feature on the tablet, she tapped the featured icon. Casper automatically went higher up in the sky; the drone began to scan all six locations at the same time. Sarah couldn't believe her eyes, she was impressed with the high-tech technology, Casper possessed. She drove out of the garage on her way to Bridgeport.

Casper scanned more and more people as they crowded around the crime scene, one of the powerful lens covered the Seaside Park explosion Casper scanned through a crowd of people in the park as they watched a lady's cell phone. Casper placed a target onto her cell phone, then zoomed in on the screen. It showed one of the victims, a black girl standing beside a baby stroller, while she talked on the cell phone, it exploded! The explosion wiped out everyone who stood near her. Casper played back, it's recording of the incident in slow motion, the footage actually showed the girl head coming apart. The impact was devastating with an eye blinded flash from the explosion. Casper immediately figured out what caused the explosion, the cellphone carried an explosive device inside it. Cell phones may have caused the other explosions, which is why everything happen in different locations. Casper scanned the cell phone; it was recognized as being a iPhone 7 manufactured by Apple.

Sarah had a shit load of information, Casper had accumulated, she drove off the Bridgeport exit, entered into the city. The place looked like a war zone; clouds of black smoke was still in the air. Sarah first stop was Main Street, she saw bricks and shattered glass everywhere along with over turned vehicles. She recognized a variety of different law enforcement officers, keeping the crowd of people and news reports at bay. Sarah displayed her F.B.I. badge, she showed it to one of the

State Police officers, he gave her a head nod. Sarah crossed underneath the yellow do not cross tape, she looked at the destroyed building. She put on her eyeglasses and the Holiday Inn slowly began to reappear, she saw a green glow on the tenth floor, which indicated the explosion happened right there. All eyes were on Sarah, she slowly walked around analyzing the demolished areas. She left the scene and headed over to the next explosion.

The court house was nothing but crumbled concrete with shards of glass everywhere. Sarah arrived, she placed the eyeglasses over her eyes and the demolished court house reappeared. She walked away, exchanged a few words with one of the grieving Police officers, he said, "My wife was in there." She left and drove to the next location which was the Police Department.

Sarah arrived making her way through the crowd. She acknowledged the State Police and brandished her F.B.I badge, she gave her the green light to get closer to the crumbled building. She put on the eyeglasses pressed a button on the side, a hologram image of the Police Department slowly reappeared. She looked around and found the green glow, it was inside a room down the hall with a sign above the entrance. It read – lost and found department.

She left the crime scene, headed to Park Avenue where a car exploded in front of a Day Care Center, shattering the windows. The first thing she asked, "is all the children safe?" A State Police officer said, "all except for the two who were inside the vehicle with their mother." Sarah slowly shook her head, the feeling of sadness came over her, a mother and her two innocent kids. She wiped a tear from her eye and placed the eyeglasses over them, a hologram image of a vehicle reappeared, it showed a green glow on the front passenger seat, which indicated someone was seated there.

Sarah walked away from the scene, a little angry and emotional. Sarah drove to Seaside Park, she pushed her way through the crowd and stopped underneath the Pavilion next to the news media, who asked the State Police officers questions. Sarah saw the yellow caution tape, blocked off the picnic area which was destroyed. She overheard a terrified witness, talking to the news reporter, the witness said, "My friend was video recording a fist fight and captured the explosion in the background of her footage. It showed a black girl talking on her cell phone and then a loud explosion could be heard, people screamed and ran.

Sarah left the park, she drove to North Avenue, where the last explosion took place. She drove into the Walgreen parking lot, exit her vehicle and walked towards a crowd of people. They all talked about what had happened, Sarah heard someone say, it was like a scene from a action movie, the city bus just blew up! Sarah put on the eye glasses for the last time, she walked out into the street, where the explosion took place. A hologram image of the city bus reappeared; It showed a green glow on the seat in the center of the bus. She left the area and headed home; she had a lot of work to do. She kept Casper in the sky, following in her direction, scanning everything in its path.

Chapter 28

Sarah was hard at work, she had all the Bridgeport Street camera footage, she knew she had to hurry up and put an end to Randy's madness. Casper had given her a big break, the drone revealed each explosion, may have been done with cell phones. Sarah watched video footage Casper had recorded, off of someone's cell phone it showed a black girl talking on her phone, then it blew up! She rewinds the video at least six times, she couldn't believe how someone would do such a horrible thing. The sick bastard used innocent people and turned them into suicide bombers, she knew someone had to see Randy. Especially, if he walked around Bridgeport and handed the cell phones out to random people.

She began to watch the street camera footage, using a divided screen mode, which allowed her to review each street camera on one monitor. Sarah was focused in front of the monitor; she wasn't going to let nothing slip by her. She watched every vehicle coming and going from the Holiday Inn, she looked at people get picked up and dropped off. She paid close attention to each cab driver and uber driver, the entire area was busy full of traffic. She finally saw something odd on screen one, a Ford pickup truck stopped in front of the hotel, she watched to see if someone was going to exit. The passenger door opened and something was dropped onto the side walk, then the truck drove away.

Minutes later, a white guy was seen, he picked the object up off the curb and walked into the hotel entrance. Sarah thought for a second…could this have been a drug deal. She rewound the footage zoomed in; the object appeared to be a cell phone. She couldn't get a clear view of the person who drove the pickup truck. Sarah caught a glimpse of his white beard, as the truck drove away. She paused the video and captured the license plate numbers; she quickly wrote down the numbers.

Screen two showed an old white man with a full white beard, she now had her eye on a suspect, she watched him walk to the bus stop. He reached inside a plastic bag then placed an object on the bench. Seconds after, he walked away, a Spanish girl approached the bus stop. She seen the object and placed it inside her backpack. Sarah saw the girl get onto the city bus.

Screen three, the same old white man, he walked along Golden Hill Street, Sarah saw him drop something on the sidewalk. She paused the footage and zoomed in; she caught a really good close-up view of him. She recognized his eyes and his salt and peppered color beard; she just couldn't remember where she seen him before. She continued watching the footage, she saw him leave a cell phone near the court house. He walked away carrying a plastic bag, moments later, a black guy appeared, she seen him pick the cell phone up. He placed it in his jacket pocket and walked inside the court house.

Screen four, showed the suspect leave a cell phone in front of the Police Department, a police officer was seen walking outside, he saw the cell phone and picked it up. He looked around, then brought it inside the police department.

Screen five, only showed the suspect carrying the same plastic bag, coming and leaving Seaside Park his pickup truck gave a clear view of the license plate.

Screen six, the pickup truck was shown getting onto the highway headed north bound.

Sarah went back to screen three, she paused the footage and zoomed in on the suspects face again. The white beard just seemed odd, it was impossible for Randy to have aged that fast and grown a full white beard. She thought to herself...is he wearing a disguise? A lot of things didn't make sense. Sarah did a quick check on the license plate; the vehicle was registered to Leroy Peterson age 71 address 3704 Amity Rd. Woodbridge Connecticut. Sarah removed herself from the kitchen counter, when it hit her, she remembered crossing paths with Randy months ago at Walgreens.

Chapter 29

Randy was in full gear, he wore a face protector shield, he adjusted he heat on the blow torch. It became so hot; he could melt metal objects and change the form. He began to operate on a shiny small circular object, which appeared to be a piece of jewelry. Music blared out of the radio speakers; whatever he was making he sure was putting a lot of time into it.

At one point he stopped and stood back from the operating table and stared at the object. He walked back to the table, this time he pointed his finger at the object, as if he wanted to touch it. Randy left the room; he came back with a small pail full of ice cubes and water. He used the pliers and picked up the small object, he looked at it one last time, before he dropped it into the ice-cold water. It sizzled, leaving a small cloud of smoke, when it touched the cold water, sinking down to the bottom of the pail.

Ten minutes later, Randy had his hand inside the water, he fished the object out. He held it in the palm of his hand, and took a closer look at his work. He smiled, while he wiped off the silver skull designed ring. He placed the ring onto his wedding band finger, he held it in the air, admiring his new creation. He reached inside his metal cabinet drawer and grabbed a metal marble sized ball. He placed it onto the operating table, Randy begins screaming the lyrics to his favorite metal band: Suffokate.

"We must make this sacrifice, and these eyes will watch you die, the accomplishment of this casualty, your hopes and dreams fade away.... I cut and rip until it explodes terminating your fucking life."

The heavy metal music had taken over him, as if Satan was whispering sweet nothings in his ear. He took off the head gear, placed it on the table. He wiped the sweat from his forehead, then left out of Satan's den. When he reached the top of the stairs, the foul odor raced laps around him. He had become immune to his hazardous way of life. He was about to exit out the backdoor, he saw the spider, it paused inside the web, as if it was trying to hide. He noticed this spider was much bigger, than the last one, so he assumed it was a female and maybe even pregnant.

Randy speared the spider this time, he left out the house, walked to his pickup truck, He grabbed a rotted deer, tossed the dead weight over his shoulder.

He carried the malodorous carcass, before he went inside, he looked in the upper corner of his door and the spider was no longer insight, the web was vacant, so he brought the carcass inside the house, Cher looked malnourished she watched Randy's every move from a distance. His abuse toward the poor dog had gotten worse.

One day he kicked Cher, after smashing her face into a small pile of feces. Randy dropped the carcass on the kitchen floor, he went back out to the truck. He forgot his treat for the dog, he grabbed a dead cat from the bed of his truck. The cat looked runover and maybe a few days old, he carried it inside the house, then he tossed it over to Cher. She looked up, then jumped over the lifeless feline and left out the kitchen.

Randy was in the living room, having himself a triple shot of whiskey, which was something he did every now and then, he took a crumbled piece of paper, out his cargo pants pocket. He unfolded the paper and next on his list was the veterans Hospital located in West Haven. He burned the paper, using his cigarette lighter, then dropped it into the ashtray. He laid back in his Laz boy chair, turned on the television, Fox61 news was on.

A female news reporter, talked about all the Connecticut bombings. She ended the segment saying, "it's all part of a terrorist act." Randy held his glass of whiskey in the air, before he guzzled it down, he said, "I'll toast to that." He felt good knowing his work was impeccable, he poured himself another triple shot of whiskey. Then he lit a cigarette and blew smoke circles in the air, he stared at the wild handwritings that covered his walls. The whiskey had him feeling tipsy at this point, he saw a blank space on the wall. He lifted himself off, the recliner chair, reached for his black permanent marker and stumbled over to the wall. He wrote **"IF we knew each other's secrets, what comforts would we find."** He staggered back to his chair and took a long drag from his cigarette, then he charged the television channel.

The television was on animal planet, Randy poured himself one more triple shot of whiskey. While he watched a pack of lions devour a large giraffe, he began spinning around with the living room ceiling, before drowsing off, he released the glass of whiskey, it fell to the floor, leaving a wide stain on the carpet.

An hour into his blackout, Randy began to twitch, he drifted away into one of his nightmares…. his Platoon was in Afghanistan on the battlefield. He was side by side with Candyman, firing their way into enemy territory. Somehow, they became trapped and caught in a crossfire. Black Cloud screamed for his soldiers to retreat! Just when they turned around, two enemy missiles made contact and blew them away. Randy woke in a cold sweat, he looked around the living room and adjusted his eyes to the light for the TV screen, where he came into eye contact with a herd of zebras, they were splashing through a crocodile infested river. Randy looked at his watch, he changed the television channel to the 11 o'clock news. A white male news reporter, talked about Acts of terror caused by ZIZI and how they were now here in Connecticut.

Randy changed the TV channel back to animal planet, he smelt the strong aroma of liquor on the side of his recliner, he looked and saw his empty glass, turned over in the center of a large stain. He lit a cigarette, took a long drag and then blew the smoke in the air. He watched four male lions stand at the edge of the river, Randy assumed it was the lions that chased the zebras into the river. All except one zebra made it across the river, the last one struggled to make it across, it played a dangerous game, of tug of war with a large crocodile attached onto its leg. Randy grabbed the whiskey bottle, guzzled what was left inside. He wiped his mouth while watching the TV screen. He was excited to see who was going to win, the zebra was snatched back into the water and the other crocodiles arrived just in time to help devour the zebra. The color of the dirty river water, instantly turned red. Randy started laughing as the lions, turned to walk away.

He stood up from the recliner and went into the kitchen so, he could have himself a bite to eat, he sat at the kitchen table and took a bite into a tough piece of deer meat. While he looked through an auto trader magazine, he thought about getting a better pickup truck. Because his red Ford F150 wasn't running like it use too, he saw a black Chevy Silverado pickup truck it was being sold in Naugatuck, Connecticut. The price was $3,500 and Randy knew it was a steal, he took the magazine with him into the bedroom, where he set his alarm clock for 8:30 am.

Chapter 30

Sarah was at home, she put together 12 profile folders of Randy Goldberg. She put together a special law enforcement unit, which consist of 12 different police officers throughout Connecticut. She felt it was the right thing to do, because of all the pain and sorrow, Randy brought to Connecticut. Sarah played her cards smart; she had all the news stations broadcast; each bombing was done by the terrorist group (ZIZI). Make the media believe people were going online and pledged to be true followers, create homemade explosive, turn themselves into suicide bombers, take the lives of innocent people.

Sarah set up a meeting with her special team, it was held in New Haven at the New Haven Police Department. She wanted every officer to be aware of who they were dealing with, she placed the 12 profile folders inside her brief case. She took a quick shower and then she got dressed, she wore a black F.B.I tactical uniform. She took the briefcase downstairs, grabbed her federal issued Glock 9, placed the weapon into her lower back holster. She released Casper into the air, she watched the drone disappear headed to 3704 Amity Rd. Woodbridge Connecticut. She got inside her vehicle, drove out the garage headed to the highway.

She drove onto the South bound on ramp, there wasn't much traffic. So, she sped up the Benz and cruised straight ahead, she turned on the stereo system, Cold as Ice by Foreigner blared out the speakers. Sarah watched vehicles as she passed by, she saw a black and blue BMW S1000R Motor cycle, coming up from behind as the bike came closer, she seen it was a female, who pushed the bike pass her. A Silver Lexus ES350 was to the left of her, she saw the female driver peek at her. Sarah thought to herself, maybe it was the uniform, a F.B.I agent driving a Mercedes Benz 550SL Coupe, down the highway or maybe she was driving with some kind of contraband. Sarah mashed the gas pedal, leaving the Lexus far behind. She drove pass a white Buick Lacrosse CX, the Buick made Sarah take a second look, she said, "Buick's came a long way." She saw the downtown New Haven exit, so she switched lanes and got off, the exit driving behind a black Cadillac Escalade.

Five minutes later, Sarah was parked near the front entrance to the Police Department. When she exits the vehicle, the first thing she saw was a train station across the street. All eyes were on her, Sarah walked up the steps, entered into the building, where she was greeted by the chief of police, they shook hands and then he escorted her into a large conference room. Sarah saw the 12-law enforcement officers, eight men and four women. She stood at the head of the room and introduced herself, as Bomb Specialist/F.B.I. agent Sarah Richardson. She explained to everyone why she put this special unit together, she said, "I feel each and every police department should have the right to help be apart in capturing the man who caused havoc here in Connecticut."

Everyone kept quiet, while Sarah spoke, she opened her brief case, then handed each officer a profile folder of Randy Goldberg. She said, "Randy Goldberg is a very dangerous man, he served time in the military, he is a bomb specialist which explains where his skills come from, he's no amateur, he dealt with many different kinds of explosive." She asked, "everyone to open their folders." Once everyone had them opened, she said, "everyone should see two photos." All the officers looked at two large color photos of Randy Goldberg, one was printed on a clear sheet, the first photo showed Randy clean shaved his scar was visible. Sarah said, "Randy, lost his left leg, the same time he received the beauty mark on his face, he is missing his leg from the knee down. A suicide bomber got a hold of him, so, he was discharged from the military, because of his disability." She took a breath and then she said, "I believe, Randy is mentally ill from all the traumatizing events, he been through as a soldier." The second photo was captured from the city of Bridgeport Street camera, digitally enhanced, transferred onto this clear sheet.

Sarah pointed out, the salt and pepper colored beard is a part of Randy Goldberg disguise, he pretends to be older than he actually is. She made one more thing clear, "he does own a foul odor." Sarah told everyone to place the clear photo over top of photo number one. Every officer was stunned at the perfect fit, both faces were the same person. Sarah said, "Randy is going by an alias name, Leroy Peterson which is the name on his driver license, it also has his place of residence – 3704 Amity Rd. Woodbridge CT.

Sarah instructed everyone to dress in plain clothes, because this is an undercover operation, she didn't want this to go wrong and Randy get away. Sarah said, "the last officers didn't follow the instructions and took matters in their own hands, all lost their lives, when the house exploded." She asked, everyone to turn the page in their profile folder, there is a digitally enhanced photo of Randy's Ford F-150 pickup truck. Sarah said, "this is the vehicle he drives around in." She closed her briefcase and before she dismissed herself from the room, she said, "Randy house is currently under surveillance by her federally issued drone known as 'Casper the friendly ghost' and as of right now his vehicle isn't in the driveway." She also advised everyone to take their time and finish reading about the profiler.

The police chief left with Sarah out the room, he escorted her out the front door. The chief couldn't help himself, he had to ask, "what year is your Mercedes Benz?" Sarah said, "2017" while she put her shades over her eyes. She got inside the Benz and drove away from the police department headed for the highway.

Chapter 31

Early the next morning, Sarah had her special unit in Woodbridge, before she sent them out in the field, she gave direct orders, which was to be careful around the house and if anyone come in contact with the suspect, she repeated, approach with caution. The suspect still hasn't returned home, his driveway was empty and there was a bunch of trash around the back gate. The house was under heavy surveillance, officers had the premises, secured. It was going to be impossible for Randy to escape this set-up.

Two officers were posed as landscapers, parked down the street, inside the white van, four officers were seated in the back, wearing bullet proof vest and holding onto assault weapons. In the house directly across the street, six officers watched the house from a first-floor window, view. Two officers were upstairs, looking through the window blinds, special issued binoculars, aimed at Randy's living room window, looking for the slightest piece of movement.

A sun shower had come over them, it rains hard for about twenty minutes and then it moved on, leaving a double rainbow in the sky. The unit waited patiently communicated through their ear pieces. A female officer, upstairs spoke into her earpiece, she said, "there is movement in the house." Everyone waited for her lead…. She reported back, it's a dog, a French bulldog to be exact.

Sarah drove down I-95 on her way to Woodbridge so, when they raid the house, she could be present to inspect the property for explosive materials. She carried this over whelming feeling about herself, Casper was still on location, hoovering above Randy's house and finally, the drone spotted the red pickup truck. Casper alerted, Sarah letting her know the suspect was approaching the location. She told her team to get ready because the suspect is on his way. Everyone grabbed their assault weapons and waited for the green light. The room became silent, as if everyone was holding their breath.

The red pickup truck drove into the driveway, they waited for Randy to exit the truck. He just sat inside the truck; a cigarette butt came flying out the driver side window. The Boston Red Sox cap was low over his eyes, he turned the truck off and sat there as if he was waiting for something or someone. A voice came over the ear piece, telling the van driver to get ready, on the count of three. Another voice started counting 1,2,3! The van drove over towards the truck, blocked it inside the drive way. The van side door, opened and the officers swarmed the truck with assault weapons drown. Randy was forced out of the truck, he was thrown to the ground, checked for weapons. The pickup truck was also searched, one of the officers compared the smell from the truck to a decomposed body. Randy was handcuffed with his hands, behind him, when he was turned over his Boston Red Sox cap came off.

Casper scanned the body on the ground in handcuffs and it didn't register, the person who drove the truck isn't Randy Goldberg. Sarah told everyone the man in handcuffs wasn't the suspect, one of the officers asked, "where is Randy?" By the look on his face, he didn't know what was going on, he told them, he was introduced to this old man by his friend, Charles, who offered to pay him to drive the truck to this address, then he said, "I even got a Boston Red Sox cap out the deal." One of the officers held the man identification card, then he said, "Earl Lancer and he stay at a homeless shelter on Hamilton and Grand Avenue." Another officer asked, "where did you meet Randy?" Earl said, "while I was collecting cans." Four other officers were searching around the house, looking in the windows, they really couldn't see too much. One of them spotted the French bulldog, a female officer stood with the back-screen door open, she saw the spider and quickly shut the door, causing the spider to hit the ground, where she stepped on it. Then said, "that was a big spider!" Everyone was in position ready to knock both doors off the hinges, but they had to wait for Sarah to arrive. She told everyone to stay in position, she was coming down the street, a voice said, "Copy."

Earl asked the officer who watched him, what was he being arrested for? The officer didn't respond, Earl knew whatever was going on, it was serious. Randy came driving a black pickup truck down the street. Randy drove pass the house, he saw the officers and then he noticed Earl hand cuffed on the ground in his driveway. Randy was a little puzzled, he couldn't believe they were actually at his house. He drove about a half of mile, down the street, then turned into someone's driveway, where he backed out, coming back towards the house. This time he had the dark tinted window down halfway.

Casper scanned the person who drove the truck, facial recognition a perfect match as being Randy Goldberg. He drove by watched Sarah exit her vehicle in his driveway. Casper alerted Sarah giving her the description of the vehicle, Randy was driving and the direction, he got on the highway headed Southbound. Sarah contacted the State trooper barracks and gave them the information so, they could prepare a roadblock somewhere to stop him. He was too far ahead, Casper followed him from up above, no matter, what, Randy was getting caught.

Sarah gave her team the greenlight to enter the house. Seconds later, the front and back door were knocked off the hinges. The officers rushed inside with assault rifles, aimed straight ahead. A foul odor stopped them in their tracks, Sarah walked in behind them, then she said, "a little odor isn't going to kill you." She told her team to check every room thoroughly! They separated headed in different directions, destroying the place. One of the female officers found the bulldog underneath the bed, the poor little dog looked like she hadn't eaten in months. She held the shivering dog in her arms.

Sarah put on a pair of latex gloves, she took a look at the malnourished dog and then called animal control. The officer outside put Earl inside the police van so, he could go and get processed at the Woodbridge Police Department. The house was disgusting, Sarah opened the deep freezer and seen a deer head, along with another frozen rodent. She stepped away from the freezer, let the door slam shut! Sarah was called into the filthy bathroom, it looked like a breeding ground full of mold and mild dew. The toilet was full of a mixture of urine and excretion, Sarah looked at the shattered bathroom mirror. She picked up one of the bottles of medication, read the label, Zoloft and by the name, she knew he was on some strong meds. She told one of the female officers to bag all the medications.

Sarah was called into the next room, everything was tossed upside down, she figured this was his bedroom, because there were porn DVDs, all over the floor. The bed mattress was disgusting Sarah knew if she looked any closer, she would see bed bugs. There was a torn poster of Uncle Sam, hanging off the wall. Sarah asked the female officer was she recording all of this? She said, "Yes". While holding the video recorder at the wall, the whole house was full of writings on the walls. One of the quotes stayed in Sarah's head…. **"Chess is war over the boards. The object is to crush the opponent's mind."** Someone yelled out, we have a basement!

Sarah walked out of the bedroom and near the kitchen was another door, it wound ed like music was coming from there, she slowly turned the knob and opened the door. South of Heaven by Slayer blasted through the dark room, she walked into the basement with caution. Sarah hand nervously reached for the string, she didn't know if she should pull it or not. So, she took a deep breath then pulled the string. The light blinked before it came on, it looked like a dungeon. Sarah saw a bunch of different tools, a blow torch stood on top of a metal table, and hung on the wall was a face protector shield, against a map of the Town of Woodbridge, Connecticut. Sarah took a closer look and seen the retirement facility was circled, there also was a calendar on the wall. She saw the month was July, which immediately made her think about the tragic event that took place on the 4th. One of the officers turned off the radio.

Sarah saw several large buckets; she automatically knew whatever was inside those containers were used to make explosive. She needed a Special Hazmat crew to remove this destructive material. Sarah was called upstairs, she was met with a female officer who held the dog, she led Sarah outside, they were greeted by animal control. The female officer handed over the startled dog to the animal control worker who wrapped the dog in a blanket, telling the dog it's going to be alright. The dog was placed inside a small kennel then driven away.

One of the male officers walked outside, showed Sarah a burnt piece of paper, he found. She took the paper and saw some of it had turned to ashes, fallen off. She tried to decipher, what was left written on the paper, she said, "this sick bastard is aiming for the Veteran's hospital!" Sarah and her team waited outside for the Hazmat crew to arrive, and clear-out the basement.

Sarah received a phone call from an unrecognized are code, a male voice identified himself as State Police officer Michael Handsberry, he told Sarah, they have her suspect in custody. He was arrested six miles ahead, after coming out the New Jersey turnpike, he crashed into a guard rail and destroyed his front wheel axle, losing a front tire. Then he told Sarah she can pick him up at the New Jersey State trooper barrack. Sarah said, "I will be down there shortly." Then hung up the cell phone. She told her team the good news! Everyone gave high fives to one another, ending the day with a mission complete! Sarah couldn't wait to watch the video footage of the chase, Casper captured.

Chapter 32

Sarah was on her way to New Jersey accompanied by a black federally issued Chevy Suburban truck that followed behind. So, she can apprehend Randy Goldberg and transfer him over into federal custody. Sarah was finally relieved knowing Randy was in custody, he couldn't hurt or do anymore damage to the city. She listened to her favorite classic Rock station; we are the champions by Queen blared through the speakers. She sang along with the song, out loud! Either, she really liked the song or she was just in a good mood, after, giving Connecticut her hard work, sweat and tears.

Both vehicles, cruised down the Fastlane on I-95, southbound. Sarah just passed New York with the black Suburban tailing behind, they crossed lanes going into New Jersey. They drove through the Jersey turnpike, which was a long ride inside a tunnel, when they came out the other end, Sarah looked for the area, where Randy crashed his truck, she finally saw a guard rail pushed back from all the other ones. She seen pieces of glass, plastic and other debris around the crash site. Sarah drove by with a little smirk on her face, she witnessed the area, where Randy was tracked down and captured.

A half hour later, both vehicles were getting off an exit, they drove another mile, then turned into a State trooper barrack. They veered to the left, followed, what the signs were instructing them to do. The vehicles had come to a stop and waited for a large gate to open; they drove down into the building. Sarah was greeted by two muscular built clean shaved men, well dressed in uniform wearing gats. The two men walked, Sarah and the four federal agents who rode in the Suburban into a holding area, where they kept all detainees.

Sarah walked along the empty cells, she looked for Randy until, the tall State Trooper said, "he is the very last cell." He walked behind Sarah with a handful of keys, one of the federal agents took out, some handcuff, with a black box in the center and a set of leg shackles. Sarah saw Randy laying on the hard-concrete bench, the State Trooper hit the bars with his keys. A head slowly looked up at Sarah and the State Trooper, she stared at the man…. As he stood up and walked towards them. Sarah looked at the State Trooper, she said, "who is this?" The State Trooper said, "your suspect." Sarah frantically said, "this is not Randy Goldberg!" She asked, the detainee his name and the man said, "Charles, Charles Selter." Sarah quickly turned away and ran towards where her vehicle was, she yelled back to the four agents, Randy Goldberg is still out there!!!!

Chapter 33

A long-exhausted day, Sarah had between the house raid and the ride to the Trooper barrack, in which she ended up, empty handed. She looked out her kitchen window gazed into the night, she couldn't believe, how close she was to capturing Randy. She went and sat back in front of her laptop, going over the footage Casper recorded of the high-speed chase. Sarah stared at the screen, watched Randy bully his way through the traffic. She saw vehicles crash into one another, while trying to move out his way.

Randy had the State Troopers beat by a half mile, Sarah kept rewinding the footage over and over again, she couldn't understand how this was possible. Until she paid close attention and realized, Casper lost sight of the truck, once it went down into the New Jersey turnpike. Casper hovered up above then continued the pursuit, when the truck came out the other end. Sarah thought for a minute, then she pounded her fist on the table. When she figured it out, Randy must have gotten out the truck, while inside the tunnel.

Sarah stood up from the kitchen table and thought about what's going to happen next. She reached for her cell phone, called the West Haven Police Department and told them to hurry up and put extra security at the Veterans Hospital, now! She rushed out the house into the garage, racing against time. She released Casper into the air, the drone headed to the VA

Hospital at high speed. Sarah got inside her vehicle, drove off, headed to the highway. She sped through traffic, until, she finally got off, the West Haven exit, making her way to the hospital.

Sarah drove up to the front entrance, she exits her vehicle. She held her badge in hand and scream, "I am a federal agent!!!" She looked around for security, she seen them, ran over and handed them, large colored photos of Randy Goldberg. She said, "be on the lookout for this individual!" She made it known, Randy was a very dangerous man, who dealt with high explosive.

Sarah yelled out to all by standers, "If you see something suspicious report it, immediately!" Casper was above scanning all pedestrians who were in the 10-block radius of the hospital. Sarah felt a lot safer, knowing Casper was on the scene to secure the hospital. Sarah walked through the hospital, she passed out photos of Randy, making everyone aware of the suspect.

The hospital was well guarded, every exit had police present and one vehicle circled the area, by the hour. Day light had come, Sarah did one last round through the hospital, before she left to go home and get some much-needed rest. Casper was left behind to surveillance the hospital.

Chapter 34

Randy was safe, he was in good hands, he persuaded the elderly couple, who saved him from his fate. During the State Trooper chase to let him stay at their resident for the night. Because he was a little shaken, after his abduction, Randy gave them some phony story about the guy in the black pickup truck, tried to kidnap him. They welcomed Randy into their home with open arms.

The elderly couple lived in Morristown, New Jersey which was a nice peaceful town. Randy sat in the couple's recliner chair; he held the remote control in his hand. He watched the news; he saw where Charles Selter crashed and was apprehended by the State Troopers. Randy told the elderly couple; they caught the guy who tried to abduct him! The pickup truck he brought was a total wreck, he lit one of the old man's non-filtered cigarettes, while he surfed through different news channels. One of them showed a photo of him and the news report said, "Randy Goldberg is a wanted man, if you see him contact the police." Randy told the elderly couple, the handsome man in the photo look like him? He asked the old lady, is he handsome or what.

Randy turned to another news channel, this channel the news reporter said, "they have the suspect from the highway chase in custody, and he is being held at the Trooper barrack. "Randy took a long drag from his cigarette; he blew circles of smoke in the air. He saw something move around inside a cage, he stood up and walked to the cage. Randy came face to face with the prettiest white rabbit, he had ever seen in his life. He smiled and touched the cage with his hand. The curious rabbit stood still, then hopped over, thinking he had food in his hand, the rabbit smelled it. Randy took one last drag from the cigarette, he opened the cage, held the rabbit in his arm.

He walked into the kitchen, opened different drawers as if he was searching for something. He looked over at the counter next to the stove, there was a wooden case with different size knife handles sticking out. Randy reached for the biggest blade, walked to the sink, he held the rabbit tightly by the ears. He cut the poor animal at the neck; blood squirted in every direction. He left the rabbit in the sink to bleed out. He wiped his hands on his shirt, grabbed the bottle of brandy and a glass, headed back into the living room.

Randy walked pass the elderly couple and sat back in the recliner chair. He poured himself a triple shot of brandy, did a toast to the elderly couple and gulped the brandy. He wiped his mouth, poured another triple shot of brandy and then said, "you old people don't talk much, do you." They were over on the love seat together with their hands tied behind them, and plastic bags taped over their heads, suffocated. Randy couldn't think of no better way to thank them for saving his life, he reclined the chair back. He watched some old news footage where the reporter talked about the bombings in Connecticut.

Randy eyes got big when he saw Sarah in the back ground amongst other law enforcement officers, The New Haven chief of police, told everyone to be on high alert, by following the campaign – If you see something, say something Sarah was on Randy's mind, he thought about when he seen her at his home. She was wearing the same black jacket with large yellow letters on the back, which read F.B.I. Randy mumbled a few words to himself, threw back his triple shot, poured himself a third, triple shot of brandy and lit another cigarette. He saw three different phone numbers come across the TV screen, the news reporter said, "here goes the numbers to contact, if you see this suspect." The photo of Randy came back on the screen, again.

Randy looked at the elderly couple, he licked his lips and then asked them, have they ever eaten rabbit meat? He waited for a response but there was none. He struggled out the chair, staggered into the kitchen. He thought to himself, it's been a while since he last gormandized a rabbit, and he could use a lucky rabbit foot.

Chapter 35

The day had begun, Sarah was still asleep, tired from the night before, laid across the bed fully dress. The sun rays coming through her bedroom blind, while she stole an extra hour of sleep. Sarah finally rolled over, stretched her arms out, yawn and then asked Alexa what was the time? Alexa said, "the time is "1:19pm." Sarah reached for her cell phone, there were no missed calls or text messages. She lifted herself off the bed, walked into the bathroom, pulled her pants down and squatted down over the toilet. She still held her cell phone in her hand, as if she was expecting a phone call. She urinated, then undressed, looked at herself in the mirror and the image she saw was stress! Sarah had bags underneath her eyes and she appeared to be a little frail.

This case had started to put some wear and tear on her, physically as well as mentally. But she was still determined to track Brandy down, at one point she wanted him in prison with the key thrown away. Now, she was thinking more like two bullets to his head.

Sarah stepped into the hot shower, she let the water run down her body. She kept her eyes closed, focused on the soothness of the water, racing from her head down to her toes. The thoughts that were going through her mind at this particular moment must be rejuvenating. She held on to the wall with both arms stretched out, her head faced downward. While the hot water from the shower head, ricochet off her. Sarah knew that a few more minutes of this would have her, reaching for her purple friend. So, she quickly exits the shower, grabbed a towel walked out the bathroom. She needed all her strength, if she was going to track down, Randy.

Sarah searched through her closet, looked for something casual to wear. Sarah got dressed, then headed downstairs for something to eat. She walked into the kitchen thinking; two egg omelet would be good. She turned on the laptop to see what Casper had accumulated over the night. Sarah didn't see nothing out of the ordinary. So, she went to the refrigerator grabbed two eggs and some cheese, then she turned on the stove, placed a pan on top. She poured herself a glass of orange juice and stood in front of the stove with spatula in hand.

Sarah cell phone began to ring, she walked over to the counter top, reached for the ringing cell phone. She held the glass of orange juice in one hand and her cellphone in the other. She answered, an unrecognized voice said, "Hello is this Bomb Specialist F.B.I agent Sarah Richardson?" She said, "Yes." A puzzled look came to her face, before she could ask who was she speaking too? The voice sad, "well this is Randy Goldberg and I have one question to ask… **Do all dogs go to Heaven?"** And then the phone disconnected. Sarah thought for a second… then she said, "the animal shelter!?!" The glass of orange juice went crashing on the floor! And right then, the animal shelter in New Haven, **Blew up!!!** Leaving a large mushroom cloud of black smoke in the air….

Chapter 36

Sarah approached the crime scene, channel 8 News was first on the scene, news reporters were all over the place, Sarah parked her vehicle near several New Haven Police cruisers. A Red Cross van was present on the scene, two fire trucks could be seen far up ahead near the explosion, smoke and burning debris could be seen at the crime scene. Sarah exits the vehicle with badge in hand, shouted out loud who she was, pushed through the crowd. The back of her jacket read F.B.I in large yellow letters, on lookers, stared as she held her badge in the air, yelling F-B-I!!!

The police were trying to keep the crowd calm, Sarah made it pass the last of the mourning crowd and up to the yellow caution tape. Where she witnesses two overturned cars and a burnt mingled school bus. The fire fighters were still attacking certain areas with water hoses, crumbled concrete was scattered all around. Sarah heard a lady tell a news 8 reporter; kids were inside the animal shelter at the time of the explosion. They were from the Bernard elementary school on a field trip.

Sarah went underneath the yellow tape, she stopped at what would had appeared to be the front of the animal shelter. She put on her eyeglasses, pressed the button and the animal shelter began to slowly reappear. She saw the shelter wasn't a large building, she spotted the florescent stain on the floor near the back of the building. Sarah walked around the building, searched all around the crime scene. When she took off the glasses, one of the police officers approached her, he looked at a small writing pad in his hand, then said, "there was 20 kids, 4 school staff and 2 employee that worked first shift at the animal shelter. The total body count was 26, the number of animals was unknown." Sarah and the officer, crossed the yellow tape leaving the crime scene, the officer continued to talk, while he followed her through the crowd, headed to her vehicle. Sarah was speechless, all she could think about was the parents of these children and the pain they must be going through at this moment.

Sarah thanked, the officer for his information before, she excused herself getting inside her vehicle. The officer walked away, but took another glance at the emblem on her vehicle. He said, "SL550 Coupe" with a smile on his face. The officer always had a fetish for luxury vehicles and the Mercedes Benz was his favorite. Sarah sat quietly behind the steering wheel, she could still hear people cry, all over the place. A stream of tears, rolled down her face, she wiped them away and said, a prayer for the dead. She started the vehicle, as she drove away, a news 8 reporter, raced through the crowd towards her, for an interview but she was gone.

Chapter 37

Randy had taken full control over the elderly couple home, he ransacked the place completely. He learnt a lot about the couple, the old man who name was Bern Carroll SR. a retired New York city police officer, and Bettie his wife, she was a retired New York city school teacher. They had older twin sons, one was in the air force and the other was a New York city police officer in Brooklyn. The family photos had been tossed all over the place, Randy found several handguns and ammunition. Bern had a stash of playboy magazines, on top of a cheap safe. Randy slammed it on the floor, twice and then stacks of money fell out. He counted just about 50 thousand cash. Randy wrote quotes on the walls, though out the house.

The last quote he wrote was in the living room, it read **"You destroy an enemy when you make a friend of him."** Randy sat in the recliner chair, the living room and kitchen began to Reek! Dried blood stained, the kitchen, Randy left his dinner plate with the rabbit remains on it. It wasn't 'road kill' ready to eat yet, somehow flies found their way into the home. They flew back and forth between the elderly couple and the kitchen. As the days, moved on the smell got worse.

Randy was in the master bedroom, upstairs, he tore out some of the Play boy centerfold posters and stuck them on the wall. He had fallen asleep after pleasuring himself, he had Playboy magazines open all around his nude body. Randy usually takes off his prosthetic leg, when he laid in bed, but for some unknown reason he kept it on. The nude model who resembled Sarah was stuck on the wall, beside a quote that read – **"Don't waste any sympathy on me. I am the happiest person alive,"** Randy finally awakened, he laid on the bed, made eye contact with the nude center fold model who resembled Sarah. He called out her name, "Sarah" as if the model on the poster was going to answer him. In his twisted mind it did, Sarah said, "do you want some more of me." Randy smiled, grabbed his erect penis and began to ejaculate again, while he stared the center fold in her eyes. He asked Sarah, will you marry me? She said, "Yes."

A half hour later, Randy was listening to some music, he grooved to, Friend of the Devil by Grateful **dead.** He was fully dress; he wore one of Bern out fits. He moved his hands as if he, played an electric guitar. A cigarette dangled from his mouth; he heard a knock at the front door. He paused for a minute, then he went to the bedroom window, peeked through the blinds. Randy saw a short chubby old lady, she walked to her vehicle, before she got inside, she looked up at the bedroom window. As if she saw someone look through the blinds. Randy thought they made eye contact, but the old lady seen nothing. She left a note on the windshield, then she got back inside her vehicle and drove out the parking lot.

Randy went downstairs to finish, whatever the flies left behind. He took in a deep breath of the stench, as he got to the bottom of the stairs. He saw the phone off the hook, walked into the kitchen and fought the flies away from his meal. He saw the maggots move around on the plate; a smile appeared on his face. He knew it was a well-prepared meal, now, and he wouldn't have it no other way. He removed the rabbit left foot, before he devours the hare. After the meal, he went back into the living room, he sat back in the recliner chair, lit a cigarette. He flicked through the TV channels and left it on, animal planet.

A bunch of sea lions flopped onto a large rock, Randy knew they were running from something and sure enough a great white shark appeared. It stayed close by, as if it knew one of the sea lions was going to fall in the water. Randy went back upstairs, packed a duffel bag, he figured when nighttime come, he would make his way back to Connecticut. When he came back downstairs, he saw the shark was gone with a pool of blood left behind.

Nighttime slowly came, Randy had already taken Bern and Bettie, wedding rings. He opened Bern's wallet and took his driver's license, placed it in his back pocket. Rand wrote one last message – **I Am Living Proof WWP.org** on the door, he opened it, carried the duffel bag to the Buick. He stopped and grabbed the note from the windshield, it read, Bettie call me, Shelly. Randy crumbled the paper, tossed it to the ground, then got inside the vehicle and placed his lucky rabbit foot, around the rearview mirror. Where it swung from a string, Randy drove out the parking lot, he put the radio on a rock station, welcome to my nightmare by Alice Cooper blared through the speakers.

Randy headed for the highway, I-95 northbound, he had no knowledge of the damage he caused in New Haven with the animal shelter explosion yet. Before he drove onto the highway on ramp, he tossed the elderly couple credit cards out the window, he had no use for any of them. Randy was on the highway leaving out of New Jersey, and into New York. He noticed how smooth the Buck enclave drove it had nice traction, he drove off the highway exit. So, he could fill the gas tank and then he got back on the highway. Randy saw dried blood around his pretty white rabbit foot, he mumbled the lyrics, can I play with madness by Iron Maiden. He turned the volume up, moved his head to the noise. He drove with both hands on the steering wheel, before he knew it, he drove into Connecticut.

Rain came down out of nowhere, Randy turned on the windshield wipers. It started to pour down, when he made it to Bridgeport. The traffic started to slow down, Randy didn't know what to think, so he sat the chrome .45 caliber pistol on his lap. He was now trapped in bumper-to-bumper traffic, the rain wasn't letting up either. He lit a cigarette and took a look around, at some of the other vehicles that were stuck in traffic. He admired two of the vehicles one was a Silver Acura TL and the other was a Blue BMW 325xi. Car horns were going off, left and right in the nasty weather. As Randy moved further down the highway, he saw a two-car crash and someone was ejected from one of the vehicles. Because he seen a blood-stained sheet, covering a body on the side of the road.

The State Police directed the traffic, once Randy passed the accident, traffic began to pick up. Randy could see the memorial bridge lights ahead. He finally drove off the downtown, New Haven exit. He traveled through downtown, made his way towards Whalley Avenue. Twenty minutes later, he turned left into the 3 Judges Motel, where he would spend the night and figure out his next move.

Chapter 38

Sarah stayed at the V.A. hospital last night, the rain came down extremely hard. So, she decided to give Casper a break, because the drone had hovered over the hospital, nonstop for days. Extra security was stationed on all floors, along with a bomb sniffing K-9 dog, at the front entrance. Sarah took a look at her wrist watch, because she had an afternoon conference meeting at the New Haven Police Department. The city was in discomfort after the animal shelter explosion. Sarah had to explain to the public, they need not to worry! The suspect was no longer in the city, she believed Rand was somewhere in another state. Especially, after his great escape underneath the New Jersey turnpike.

The animal shelter explosion was caused by a dog that was rescued from the suspect home. There was a device implanted inside the dog, which should had been detected, before the animal left the premise. Sarah went to the cafeteria and ate breakfast, two nurses were seated behind her, Sarah could hear them, conversate about the animal shelter bombing. And how some per-schoolers were killed in the explosion. Sarah finished her breakfast, then she wiped her mouth with a napkin. She glanced at her watch again, before she took one last tour through the hospital. Sarah noticed shift change had a lot more movement in the day time. She completed her rounds, everything appeared to be intact. She stopped and had a quick chat with one of the K9-unit officers.

On her way out the front entrance, Sarah thought to herself, Randy would have to be the invisible man, in order to penetrate this security. Outside, one of the police officers asked Sarah was she coming back tonight? She responded back, yes. She got inside her vehicle and drove out the parking lot. Sarah turned on the stereo, Edge of Seventeen by Stevie Nicks, blared through the speakers. She started to sing along, while she waited for the light to change green. She grabbed her F.B.I cap off the passenger seat.

Moments later, Sarah parked in front of the New Haven Police Department, she saw three different news stations, setting up their equipment. She exits her vehicle, swiftly made her way pass the reporters, questions were being asked, but Sarah kept moving forward. She disappeared inside the front door. A police officer walked out, he told all the reporters, five minutes. Sarah and the Police chief Walked ahead of the other officers, they exit the doors, stopped in front of the news reporters. People from the community began to crowd around the steps, hoping to get answers about the tragedy.

The chief of Police spoke first, he really couldn't explain much. So, Sarah went ahead first, she stated her full name, Sarah Richardson and then her occupation, Bomb Specialist/ F.B.I. agent. After, she displayed her credentials, she explained her theory about the animal shelter explosion. The crowd of people stood silently, listened to Sarah speak, every channel showed this Special News Report. The Indian man who gave Randy the key to his room, last night, he ate a bagel while watching, the Special News Report, he waited for the police to show a description of the suspect.

Randy rushed out the bathroom, when he heard Sarah's voice on the television. He didn't even wipe his behind, nor did he flush the toilet. The unpleasant smell followed him into the room, he stared at the television, while he reached for a cigarette. He noticed News 8 was being broadcast live in front of the New Haven Police Department. He paid the crowd no mind, all he saw was Sarah cute face, she wore her F.B.I. cap, speaking to the people. Randy began to get dressed his psychotic mind took over his world. He couldn't take his eyes off, the love of his life. The dark flower printed, mildew stained, curtains had years of wear and tear.

The duffel bag was on the floor, stacks of cash peeked out, the chrome .45 caliber pistol, rested in between two pillows at the head of the bed. After, Randy struggled with his suspenders, he checked his pockets. As if he lost something and then he pulled out a wedding ring. He went closer to the old Zenith colored TV screen, he got down on one knee and anxiously asked Sarah would she marry him? Sarah pointed towards a Fox61 News reporter, who begin asking her questions? Sarah answered then pointed to another news reporter, she raised a photo of Randy Goldberg towards the crowd. She told everyone this is the person, responsible for the bombing. He is number one on the F.B.I. most wanted list.

The Indian man lean forward in his chair, stared at the photo, like he had been in contact with the suspect. Randy grabbed his car keys off the nightstand, he left out the door, getting inside the Buick enclave, Dirty women by Black Sabbath played on the radio. Randy was on his way to the New Haven Police Department, he drove down Whalley Avenue. He seen a white BMW X-6 and when he drove pass, he noticed two kids in the back seat, they both held tablets in their hands.

Randy turned the stereo volume up, Dark moves of love by M83, blasted through the speakers. When he made it to the police Department, everyone was gone. Except a couple of news reporters who were getting inside, separate trucks. Randy spotted Sarah Blue Mercedes Benz SL550 Coupe still parked out front. So, he parked his vehicle and turned down the stereo volume. He decided to wait for her to come out. Two songs later, he saw Sarah being escorted out the front entrance. By the chief of police who shook her hand. Randy watched her walk down the stairs, but inside of his sick mind, Sarah was moving in slow motion. She got inside her vehicle, when she drove off, Randy left following behind.

Chapter 39

Sarah was in a deep sleep, dreaming about rescuing people from a hospital explosion. While she was directing a group of people out the hospital, another bomb exploded, on an upper level. As the building crumbled down, Sarah's amazon alarm clock started to go off, she quickly stuck her head from underneath the comforter, looked around in the dark bedroom. The only light was coming from the TV screen, Sarah had fallen asleep, while she watched a Bruce Lee movie. She told Alexa, she was awake, the alarm clock instantly went silent. Sarah laid in the bed, she looked at the ceiling, she had a long night at the hospital and then her afternoon, conference meeting at the New Haven Police Department. It had taken a toll on her, she knew the only time she usually dream, was, when she was really tired.

Randy had Sarah working overtime, he was like an evil spirit that constantly tormented her. Sarah got out the bed, she went into the bathroom to urinate. Then she splashed the sink water on her face, before she brushed her teeth and rinsed her mouth. She walked back into the bedroom, turned on the lights. She peeked through her blinds; nighttime came fast. She got dressed, and then she went into her closet, grabbed a small firearm, which was a Glock .40 handgun. She placed her F.B.I. badge around her neck, she reached down on the floor by her bed, grabbed some panties and other items. She dropped the panties inside the dirty clothes hamper. She went downstairs to grab a bite to eat, before she headed to the hospital.

Sarah cell phone began to ring, she answered the call, it was a Police officer at the hospital, he wanted Sarah to come now, because a suspicious package had been found. Sarah told the officer in charge not to touch the box and keep everyone away from it! Sarah rushed out the house got inside her vehicle, when the garage door opened, she drove out heading to the street. Sarah front headlights, shined on a Black Buick enclave that was park directly across the street. The bright headlights woke up Randy, he watched Sarah turn right onto the street and speed towards the highway. She disappeared into the night; Randy sat inside his vehicle for a few more minutes. Sarah's street was pitch black, there were no light poles insight. Randy reached inside the glove compartment, he put a small object into his pocket. Some headlights were coming behind him, the vehicle drove by. He exits his vehicle and crossed the street walking towards Sarah house.

Randy walked around the back of her home, he stood at her back door. The sensor light came on, making it easy for him to penetrate the door lock. He reached inside his pocket, pulled out a small lock-pick he retrieved from the elderly couple's home. Randy opened the screen door and stuck the device into the backdoor lock. He moved the device in a up and down motion, until, he heard a click sound, which indicated the door was unlocked.

He slowly turned the door knob, then he walked inside with a smile on his face. He found the light switch and when the lights came on, Randy was standing the kitchen. The first thing he saw was an empty TV dinner tray on top of the full trash can, next to a blue bin with empty water bottles. There was another door, he opened it and it was to the garage. So, he shut the door and walked into the living room. He looked around and went to a large bookshelf, he finger scrolled through some book titles. He stopped at a book titled: The New England Grimpendium – A guide to Macabre and Ghastly Sites by J.W. Ocker. Randy thought to himself, the book seems interesting, he pulled it off the shelf and read the blurb. He placed the book back inside it's slot, he walked towards a large leather sectional.

He felt like a kid wandering around in Disney World. Inside one room he came across on the first floor had a lot of luggage. Randy gently went through all of them. He leant Sarah clothes size as well as her taste for designer shoes.

Randy went upstairs and walked into the master bedroom. While looking around, he noticed a picture frame on the night stand. Randy grabbed the frame staring at an unfamiliar face. It wasn't Sarah but she looked cut, possibly Latina. He placed the picture back on the night stand. He walked over towards the television. Where he picked up a Bruce Lee DVD box-set. Randy thought back when he use to watch Bruce Lee movies overseas. He sat on the bed admiring the softness of the mattress.

Randy laid back stretching himself out, he couldn't believe it, he was finally home. Randy rolled around on the bed. He begins smelling the sheets and comforter. Randy paused when he seen the bathroom, letting go of the comforter. He got off the bed and went walking into the bathroom. Randy went straight for the dirty clothes hamper which was like finding buried treasure. He found a pair of panties, underneath two towels and a sports bra, Sarah dropped inside the treasure chest. Before she left the house.

Randy mouth begin to water…. as he put her panties to his nose. He inhaled and the tang from Sarah vagina raced up his nostril. Randy stared at himself in the bathroom mirror. He held the panties with both hands to his nose. He finally got himself a taste of what he'd been waiting for...

Sarah exits her vehicle hurrying inside the hospital. Two officers had directed her to a large package. Sarah noticed it was shipped from Amazon. She put on her eye glasses and press the on button. The items inside the box appeared, Sarah slowly walk around the box without touching it. There was no sign of any explosive device. She yelled out, "Clear!" Before, reading the label then told the officers the package belongs to a Doctor by the name of Melody Bernat on the seventh floor....

Randy went walking down the stairs, he was still holding onto Sarah panties. He went back to the bookshelf and took the book that had interest him. And then, silently left back out, the back door. Carrying the book in one hand and her panties in his other. While he walked to his vehicle.

Inside of Randy's sick mind he was walking with Sarah to the parked vehicle. He went to the front passenger side, unlocking the door. Randy asked Sarah to hold the book.... He places the book on top of the panties on the seat. He pulled the seat belt and locked it. As if he was securing Sarah in the seat. Randy shut the car door and then he got inside the driver seat. He starts the vehicle while looking at the panties. Telling Sarah, he was going to take good care of her. He drove off turning on the stereo. A skull full of maggots by Cannibal Corpse was playing. Randy was driving down the highway holding the steering wheel with both hands. Every now and then he would cut his eyes at Sarah. Making sure she was comfortable. She just sat quietly with a smile on her pretty face.

The Indian man looked out the front office window. He watches Randy drive into the 3 Judges motel. The motel parking lot was still full. Even after the drug raid that took place on the second floor. Randy found a park right in front of his room door. He sat in the vehicle for a few minutes talking to Sarah. He told her they were going shopping tomorrow for a wedding dress and Tuxedo. After their conversation Randy exits the vehicle. He went to the passenger side, where he helps Sarah out of her seat belt. When Randy opens the room door, the foul odor came rushing at him. Randy held Sarah hand as they walk inside the room. He places the book on top of the night stand. He led Sarah into the toxic bathroom.

Where they both stripped naked. Randy came walking out the bathroom. He was wearing Sarah panties. He pushes everything off the bed wand then he laid down with his erect penis bulging out the side of the panties. Randy begins ejaculating with his eyes closed. Sarah was in charge of the situation. She was bouncing up and down, screaming how she love him!!! Until, Randy released his semen all over himself. He rolled over and they went to sleep.

Chapter 40

The police were setting up, they were in full tactical gear. The parking lot was full of law enforcement. One of the officers held his hand in the air. He yelled out 3,2,1 and a battering ram knock down the front door. The police officers all stopped in their tracks. When they caught a whiff of the decomposing bodies. One of the officers said, "we going to need face mask before entering inside here." Another officer began throwing up…. People were looking out their living room windows. Trying to figure out what in the hell was going on. One elderly couple said, "they smelt death somewhere around here."

A homicide vehicle drove into the parking lot. One of the police officers block the entrance with his squad car. Eight police officers wearing face mask went inside the apartment. They were looking for an elderly couple by the mane of Bettie Carroll and her husband Bern Carroll Sr. Shelly who was a friend of Bettie filed a missing person complaint.

Two of the officers were moving the front door from the entrance. They notice the writing **I Am Living Proof** <u>www.org</u> on the door. One of the officers took pictures of it. And then went moving along in the home. Four officers were standing around the two decomposed bodies. The plastic bags had been cut from their heads. It was confirmed that they were the elderly couple. One officer said, "it looks like death by suffocation." Two officers were taking pictures of the two bodies. A female officer pointed at their hands. She notices their wedding ring fingers were missing. A lot of camera flashing was going on… The living room television was on the animal planet channel. The living room was a mess. An officer was pointing to a quote written on the wall that read – **You destroy an enemy when you make a friend of him.**

Another officer said, "what kind of sick bastard would do such a thing like this…" four police officers were in the kitchen. Where dried blood stains were everywhere. They found an unrecognized animal skull. A female officer yelled out here goes an empty rabbit cage! The rabbit remains were found on a dinner plate. The officers hadn't noticed it was missing a limb. Flies had laid eggs on everything, causing maggots to take control of all the infested areas. Another female officer was taking pictures in the kitchen. She said, "it looks like the rabbit may have been eaten." Music could be heard coming from upstairs. Three officers went slowly up the stairs with their weapons drawn.

The whole upstairs was a wreck… An officer kicks the bedroom door open!

War pigs live the evil album version by Black Sabbath was playing. The bedroom looks like a hurricane came through it. Because everything was toss all over the place. There was a quote written on the wall. It read **Don't waste any sympathy on me. I am the happiest person alive.** Along with some playboy centerfold posters. There were photos of the two victims and their family scattered on the floor. One officer said, "the deceased couple had twin boys."

One was a NYC police officer and the other son was in the Air Force. A female officer said, "the elderly couple had raised good sons and it was going to hurt them. When they get this phone call…" This was the first atrocious crime ever in Morristown, New Jersey. The place where people could retire and grow old.

Chapter 41

The V.A. Hospital received two phone calls with a male voice saying he was going to blow up the building. Sarah orders the security team to keep this information quiet. She didn't want to startle the people. Sarah knew it was a copycat pretending to be Randy. He would never call without saying some kind of weird quote or something. Sarah couldn't take any chances either. She went to her vehicle and open the trunk. Taking Casper out Sarah program the drone. Using the multiple lens feature. Some lady walking her two kids watch Sarah release Casper into the air. The drone went straight up then it disappeared hovering above the hospital.

One of the kids was pointing up at the sky. He asks his mother could he have one? Thinking Casper was some kind of toy. Sarah grabbed the tablet and smiled at the kids. She went back inside the hospital. Casper was on high alert. Sarah grabbed the tablet and smiled at the kids. She went back inside the hospital. Casper was on high-alert. When Sarah turn-on the tablet. She seen Casper hard at work. The drone had a 20-mile radius. It was scanning every person, place and vehicle. Sarah was doing a walk through on the seventh floor. When she ran into Dr. Melody Bernat.

A tiny petite older white woman. She resembled Judge Judy in the face. Dr. Melody Bernat apologized for the commotion with her package. Sarah said, "no problem." They shook hands then Sarah went towards the stair well. While Sarah was walking to the eighth floor. She took a look at her tablet and then the time. Sarah hadn't plan on being at the hospital this long. She was ready to leave, Casper wasn't gonna let nothing get by. A short time later, Sarah made it back to the first floor. She went into the lady's bathroom to use the toilet. Sarah sat in the stall. Watching Casper scan everything around the hospital. She felt more secure with having Casper on the job.

Minutes later, Sarah was letting the next shift officers know she's about to leave. Sarah most definitely could use some rest. When she made it to her vehicle? Some lady ran over to her… The lady told Sarah a red pickup truck just dumped something on West Spring Street! Sarah couldn't take any chances. She left the lady by her vehicle. Sarah walks towards West Spring Street. It was a street on the side of the hospital.t Sarah begin looking for anything suspicious. She came across a broke microwave. The front window was shattered and the cord was gone. Sarah told the lady someone toss their junk on the side of the street and it was a broken microwave. The lady said, "Sorry." Sarah told her, don't be sorry because if you see something, say something.

Sarah got inside her vehicle. She sat there for a minute. Watching the tablet, Sarah made the footage rewind to when the red pickup truck took the right turn onto West Spring Street. She seen someone toss the microwave out the passenger window. Sarah zoom-in and notice it was a female. She then zoom-in on the license plate (8134F1). Sarah drove out the parking lot… She was heading to the highway. She wanted to take a nice hot shower and relax. Sarah drove into Hartford; she made a quick stop at Dunkin Donuts.

A few minutes later, she was getting out her vehicle in the garage. Sarah walks inside the house. A faint odor took her by surprise. The kitchen light was on… Sarah thought maybe she left it on last night. When she rushes out the house, she looks at her trash can and seen it was full. Sarah took off her shoes making herself comfortable at the kitchen counter. She begins eating her two croissants. Sarah finished her food; she went into the living room. Where the same smell was lingering, she told Alexa to remind her to take the trash out tomorrow morning. She sat on the leather sectional her cell phone began ringing. Sarah answered it saying hello. She recognized the female voice. It was a good friend of hers, F.B.I. agent Courtney Weatherly. She was told to contact Sarah because of the similarity in their cases.

Courtney begins telling Sarah about her murder case in Morristown, New Jersey. She got graphic with the details, explaining how the suspect dismembered the victims wedding ring fingers. And how their pet rabbit was savagely mutilated. Possibly, eaten by the suspect. What caught Sarah attention was when she mentions, there were quotes written on the walls. Courtney and Sarah went back and forth sharing information about the suspect. Sarah became convinced that the suspect was indeed Randy Goldberg. Before they hung-up… Courtney said, "the suspect was possibly driving around in the victim's vehicle. Which was a black Buick Enclave with New Jersey Plates."

Sarah stood up walking pass the large bookshelf. She didn't even notice the empty book slot. She went upstairs walking into her bedroom. Before she stripped out of her clothes heading into the bathroom. Turning on the shower, the mist from the hot water quickly made its present known by covering the bathroom mirror.

Chapter 42

Alexa woke up Sarah reminding her to take out the trash. After Sarah put the trash on the curb, she went on her morning job at the park. Which was a place she had been neglecting for quite some time. Ever since Randy lead her on a cat and mouse chase. He had no respect for the human life! Sarah dedicated her life to putting an end to his mayhem. She was on her fifth lap jogging around a group of thick women. Who were speed walking around the track? Sarah didn't know each time; she went pass them. She made them remember how their bodies once was... Sarah grabbed her towel from around her neck. She begins jogging in place, while she wipes the sweat from her face. Sarah took a quick look at her fit bit. All her vitals were looking really good, showing healthy signs! She realized that her morning jog was a great stress reliever. Sarah said, "fuck it!" She decided to run three more laps.

Sarah made it to her house. She was in the kitchen making herself a healthy breakfast. Sarah sat at the counter eating her scrambled egg-whites with toast. She set-up a get together with Courtney. They both agreed to meet in New York at the Manhattan Ocean Club. Which was an expensive seafood restaurant located in the Theater District. Sarah untied her top knot and step into the running shower for a quick wash. She got dress standing in front of her large bedroom mirror. She wore a blue one-piece pant suit with her nude colored nine-west leather pumps. Before Sarah left out the house, she put one of the favorite Glocks inside a blue leather clutch.

Sarah loved the pistol, because it was light-weight and easy to tote around. She drove out the garage, taking her vehicle for a quick car-wash. She had the tablet on the passenger seat, in case Randy was spotted. Sarah left the car-wash her Benz was gleaming in the sun. She seen some lady standing on the side walk, picking up her dog's poop. Sarah made it onto the highway. She turns on her stereo Hit me with your best shot by Pat Benatar was playing. Sarah had always been a fan of her. Every since the hit single – Love is a battle field. She was singing along, pushing her SL550 through traffic.

Sarah blue Benz was a head-turner. She drove pass an Infiniti QX80 and the gentleman who was driving. Sarah couldn't tell if he was looking at her or the Benz. She just gave him a little smile. Sarah found herself side by side with a Mercedes Benz GLC3004-Matic. She sped up passing the SUV. When Sarah Drove into New York the traffic start getting crazy. She drove pass two accidents and a broke down box-truck. Sarah drove into Manhattan.

She voice activated the GPS and then she said, "Manhattan Ocean Club." A map of the area appeared on the screen along with all the street names. Sarah's location was W.58 Street in-between Fifth and Sixth Ave. She was in the area when she received a call from Courtney. She asks Sarah was she there yet? Sarah said, "five minutes away." Courtney said, "me too." They both met inside the parking garage around the corner from the restaurant. Courtney got out a Silver Audi A4 Quattro. Sarah gave her a hug, Courtney told Sarah she hasn't changed a bit. Sarah said, "you either." While admiring Courtney's black chic jumpsuit. Courtney led the way around the corner.

The ladies turn heads, as they pass by a small group of men. Who were leaving the restaurant after their business meeting? Sarah and Courtney took the complements as they walk inside. It was a nice elegant seafood restaurant. They were met by a waitress who escorted the ladies towards the back. The waitress then hands them two menus. She walks away from their table. Giving them time to go through the menus. Sarah was looking at her menu. There was a variety of seafood platters to choose from… Crab cakes, Cold Poached Salmon and grilled Sword Fish.

Courtney had eaten at this restaurant numerous times. She knew what to order. Her favorite grilled Salmon Steak with Cole Slaw and steamed Potatoes. Sarah decided to try the grilled Red Snapper with Cole slaw and rice. The both decided on a glass of some California white wine. The ladies had small talk, while waiting for their food. Catching up on each other lives.

Courtney had graduated from the academy a year before Sarah. They both realized ain't much changed. Work was work especially in their line of profession. There entrees arrived with two chilled glasses of white wine. The ladies begin eating their food. Sarah notices a gentle man trying to get her attention. She seen his date walking to the lady's room. Sarah just ignored his flirts, taking a sip of her wine. Courtney forgot to let Sarah know the men in here were very flirtatious. After their meals, they shared more information about Randy.

Sarah told Courtney his whole life story and how she almost captured him. Courtney said, what kind of person would suffocate an elderly couple, trash their home and leave bizarre writings on the walls. Sarah looked at Courtney then she said, "A Sick Psycho-Path by the name Randy Goldberg!" An hour had gone by, Sarah and Courtney wrapped up their meeting. They left the restaurant walking to the parking garage. The

Tyrone Harvey

ladies had one last embrace before getting in their vehicles. The Mercedes Benz followed behind the Audi A4, driving out the parking garage.

Sarah drove to this shoe store on 7ᵗʰ Ave called Shoe Parlor. She brought two pair of Carum wedge sneakers. While she was in line at the cash register. Sarah thought she seen Randy walk by... She left out the store following behind him. When she reaches for her hand gun. He turns around at the sound of Sarah heels. She seen his face. It wasn't Randy, she almost pulled her gun out on an innocent pedestrian. Sarah eased her hand out of the clutch purse. She turns around and went back to the shoe store. Sarah paid for her sneakers; she left the store getting inside her vehicle. She drove off listening to Faith by George Michael.

Sarah made it onto the highway driving through the rough traffic. A black Buick Enclave drove pass her. Sarah looks at the license plate, it was a New Jersey plate. She followed the vehicle through traffic. When Sarah drove along side of the SUV, she noticed it was a black couple inside. Sarah had an uncomfortable ride home.

There was so many black Buick SUV's on the highway. She was driving herself crazy. Sarah finally made it home, she brought her shopping bag inside the house. She went upstairs changing into one of her uniforms. Sarah had the seafood breathe, she went into the bath room and gurgled some mouth-wash. She went downstairs and left out the house. Sarah sat inside her vehicle. Looking at the tablet, waiting for the garage door to completely open. She places the tablet on the passenger seat. And then she turn-on the stereo, driving out the garage on her way to the hospital. Listening to Hotel-California (Live version) by the Eagles.

Chapter 43

Randy was on an early morning mission. He went to two different used car dealerships. Trying to trade in the Buick Enclave for a different vehicle. He found a used car dealership in North Haven. The old white man was happy to take the vehicle off Randy hands. He gave Randy a Silver Honda HR-V. Randy knew it was a matter of time. Before the police everywhere start looking for the Buick. Randy was driving down Dixwell Ave. He was on his way to Home Depot. He needs a few more items, he drove pass two Hamden Police officers. They had a Black Buick Enclave pulled over.

Randy went into the Home Depot parking lot. He sat for a minute and then he exits the SUV. When he walks inside the sliding doors, a young white kid who was wearing a red Home Depot vest, offered to help Randy, who decline his offer. Randy grabbed a carriage and push on down the aisle. He already knew what he was looking for and where to find it.

While Randy was waiting in the long line. He was wondering if Sarah was still asleep. Some old man was in front of Randy with three kids. They must have been his grand kids. One of them took a roll of duct tape out of Randy carriage. The old man told the kid to put it back! The kid dropped it back inside the carriage. Randy just smiled while waiting patiently in line. He seen two of the other kids put something in their pockets. The older looking kid seen Randy watching. He put his finger in front of his mouth. Which was a signal for Randy to keep quiet. Rand finally made it to the register. He paid for his items with cash. Randy left out the store. He opens the back of his SUV and place the items inside.

Randy drives back to the motel. It wasn't many vehicles there in the day time. He noticed an Indian woman was working. She was sweeping the front office entrance. Randy didn't care he had a lot of work to do. He opens the back of his SUV, bringing the bags inside the room. The Indian woman was being nosey Randy just gave her a smile and a hand wave. She smiled back, then turn around walking into the office.

Randy shut the door, he seen the panties on the bed. The same way he left them. He put the last bag on the floor. (In his sick mind) Randy went over to Sarah and gave her a kiss. She turns around stretching her arms, smiling at him. Randy asks Sarah if she wanted to help him put two pressure cooker bombs together? Sarah leans up with an excited look on her pretty face. She said, "Yes!" Randy gave her another kiss and then he starts taking everything out of the bags. He places each item on the floor side by side. As if they had to be in a certain order.

Sarah was leaning over his shoulder. She was watching him put his creation together. Randy ask Sarah could she hand him the nails. Sarah grabbed the box and shook them. Before she passes them to him. Sarah became wet in between her legs. She whispered in Randy's ear. Telling him she was horny and wanted to have sex again! Randy went into the bathroom and when he came out. He was naked wearing the panties.

Chapter 44

Sarah made it home around noon-time. Last night wasn't as bad as the other night with all the prank calls. She was in the kitchen looking for something to cook. Sarah was mad she didn't get another order to go. When she was at the Manhattan Ocean Club. She said to herself… "Courtney done introduced her to a new seafood restaurant." Sarah took one of her Stouffer TV dinners out the freezer. She read the label it was a Kentucky Bourbon Glazed Chicken dinner. Grilled white meat chicken and pecans in a Bourbon sauce with roasted sweet potatoes. Sarah carried her dinner over to the microwave. She opens the door and put the tray inside. She shut the door and press 20minutes on the touch pad. The tray start going around in the micro-wave. Sarah went back to the refrigerator opening the freezer again. She found what she was having for dessert. Ben and Jerry's caramel cookie fix ice cream.

Sarah went into the living room, where she smelled that same faint odor. She thought about her trash can… then ignored the smell. She wiped her finger across the large book shelf. Searching for any signs of dust. The New England Grimpendium: A guide to Macabre and Ghastly sites by J.W. Ocker was back in its slot. Sarah had no idea Randy was in and out her house while she was working nights at the hospital.

Sarah grabs the TV remote control and turn-on the television. She sat on the sectional waiting to hear the bell on the microwave. So, she could eat… The TV was on animal planet Sarah didn't even question herself about how her TV was on that channel. She just watches a roadrunner devour a snake. And just when the bird swallowed the snake. The micro wave bell went off! Sarah grabs the remote control. She turns off the television. She walks into the kitchen. Smelling her Stouffer's dinner through the microwave. She grabs an oven mitten and took her dinner out. Bringing it over to the counter, she peels the plastic seal from the top of the tray. The glazed chicken aroma took over the entire kitchen.

Sarah sat there eating her dinner. She wonders what was Randy's next move going to be… Sarah heard the neighbor kids in the back yard. She took a peek through the blinds. She seen them playing kick ball. Sarah finishes her dinner, throwing the empty tray into the trash can. She grabbed the ice cream out the freezer. She took it upstairs with a spoon. She changed into something more relaxing.

Sarah put in her Bruce Lee's Game of Death DVD. She climbs into her bed, watching the movie. While she ate her ice cream. Sarah thought about the black Buick Enclave, Randy was supposed to be riding around in…. for a second. Then Bruce Lee took full control. Sarah eyes became glued to the television screen. She dozed off for a while, when she opens her eyes Bruce Lee was wearing a yellow sweat suit with black stripes down both sides. He was fighting some tall blind black guy played by Kareem Abdul Jabbar. Sarah reach for her ice cream, she forgot it was all gone.

The Ben and Jerry cup was empty with a spoon inside. When the movie finish, Sarah grabbed her cell phone. She gave Courtney a call to see how she was making out with her case. Courtney phone went to voice mail. So, Sarah hung up thinking she was busy. Minutes later, Courtney called Sarah phone. She asks Sarah what's up? Sarah said, "she was wondering how was her case coming along." Courtney said, "the finger prints came back and they were 100% Randy Goldberg's." Sarah ask Courtney did she get one of those drones the company came out with? Courtney said, "the drone with facial recognition." Sarah said, "Yes." Courtney said, "the same day she was assign to the case". The drone was actually hovering around the Morristown area of New Jersey.

Looking for any signs of its target. Which is Randy Goldberg and the stolen black Buick Enclave. Courtney told Sarah when they left the seafood restaurant. She was being followed by some light skin dude, who was driving the same Mercedes Benz SL550 coupe. Sarah had except his was Silver. Courtney said, "she pulled over at a rest stop. She held her .38 special down, while she rolled down the window." Courtney asks the man could she help him? The man said, "he wanted to chat with her at the seafood restaurant. But when he came out the men's restroom, we were gone...". He asks for Courtney number? She rolled up her window and drove off. Sarah and Courtney start laughing... Then Sarah said, "You did say the men in there were flirtatious."

Before they hung up... Courtney told Sarah next time she was gonna take her to this other seafood spot called Atlantic Grill located on the east side on 3rd Ave near 77 Street. Sarah got out the bed and changed the DVD, she put Bruce Lee's Fist of Fury in the DVD player. She ran downstairs for a quick snack. Sarah came back upstairs carrying a bag of chocolate chip cookies, the soft ones.

She climbs back in the bed. Watching Bruce Lee kick some butt... half way through the movie Sarah was curled up asleep with the movie watching her.

Chapter 45

Randy was putting all his belonging into his SUV. When he finished packing the vehicle, he went back into the room. He took Sarah by her hand and walk her out to the truck. She told Randy his new truck was nice and she like the color. Randy opens the passenger door and put the panties on the seat. Then he secured the seat belt around her.

Randy was very protected over Sarah. She had somehow won over his cold heart. Randy made one quick run inside the room. He hid one of his pressure cooker bombs' behind the front door. So, when the house keeper open the door, she won't see it. Randy carried the other one over near the front office entrance. He got inside his truck, giving Sarah a kiss and they drove from the 3 Judges Motel. Randy turns on the stereo – a lullaby for the devil by Dead Soul Tribe was on the radio.

The pressure cookers had timers on them. Nobody was going to survive…. What was about to happen. Randy and Sarah were riding down Whalley Ave. The Indian man was drinking a coffee. While he talks to his wife, he had their three daughters with him. They were watching the television. One of the maids went upstairs and one went straight to Randy's empty room. When she opens the door, a foul odor chased her. As she stumbled backwards with her shirt over, her nose. Which didn't help much because she starts puking! Five seconds later, the first explosion went off, followed by the second one. The 3

Judges Motel was nothing but a bunch of crumbled concrete and burning rubble. People at the gas station drove away from the scene. While other people ran across the street. Because the gas station caught on fire. All the gas pumps were shooting fire into the air. Moments later, the fire trucks had arrived. There was no saving the Motel it was demolished! The Police had the streets blocked off... People at the Regal Inn Motel across the street were frighten. They didn't know if their Motel was next. The Police had them, trapped across the street. Nobody could come or leave from over there. News 8 was first on the scene. They were setting – up down the street, the camera man had a clear shot of the gas – station inferno. People were pulling over asking the news reporter what was going on? Nobody knew nothing all they heard was two loud explosions. One after the other. People living out West Hills housing complex heard the explosion.

Some people thought an airplane had crashed around here. NBC and Fox61 had arrived on the scene. They were setting up beside the News 8 truck.

They were asking the crowd questions? A person told NBC a UFO crashed down the street. Landing on the 3 Judges motel. Fox61 was asking the crowd questions? No one had any answers to give them. People just spoke about the loud explosion! The fire fighters finally killed the fire. They were still spraying some hot spots. Making sure the fire wouldn't start back up.

Sarah arrived on the scene. She parks her vehicle next to a few police cruisers. She exits the vehicle wearing her F.B.I. cap and jacket with the large yellow letters on the back. The female reporter from News8 spot Sarah first. She went towards Sarah who decline to talk with any of them. Right now, she was trying to figure out, a way to get by all these people. So, she can get closer to the crime scene. Sarah pulled out her, badge holding it in the air. As she walks down towards the fire fighters. She asks the fire department chief what happened. He said, "the same thing everyone else did" All he could recall was two loud exploding sounds! Sarah didn't know what to scan first.

She figured where the motel once stood had the most damage. She put on her eye glasses. The 3 Judges Motel begin to appear... Sarah seen a fluorescent green stain near the front office. Then she spots another one inside the room close to the gas station. Which explains how the gas station caught on fire. Sarah walks over to the fire chief. She told him what caused the explosion and why the gas station went ablaze. The fire chief was amazed at how she figured all this out. Sarah advised him to go share the information with the police chief. So, he could address it to the public and news media.

Sarah stood with the police chief while the reporters ask questions. Everybody begins asking questions at the same time. The police chief yelled out one at a time! He pointed to the female News8 reporter. She asks what caused the explosion? The police chief said, "a home-made bomb…. Possibly a pressure cooker." The male Fox61 reporter asks do he have any suspects? The police chief said, "no suspects at this time." The female NBC reporter asks is this the work of serial bomber Randy Goldberg? The police chief paused before he answered… He said, "not to his knowledge." Sarah went to her vehicle, she sat inside debating with herself. Wondering was this the work or Randy or not? Randy would have called 911 and told the dispatcher some kind of quote. The police chief walks over to Sarah, vehicle. He leans down telling her it was the work of her suspect.

Because he called the police department and he said, **"Don't let one act of evil, ruin your view of the world."** Then he hung up the phone.

The dispatcher took it as a prank caller. She didn't see any red flags. It was now conformed! Sarah knew for sure that Randy was back in Connecticut!!! Sarah left the crime scene. When she drove onto the highway, she turns on the stereo – One Way or Another by Blondie was play... Sarah turns up the volume. She begins thinking to herself... how was she going to catch this son of a bitch!!! Sarah made it home, she was on the phone. Telling her security team to be on high-alert! Because her suspect was back in town.

She knew she couldn't catch Randy alone. So, she made one last phone call to Courtney. Letting her know Randy was back in Connecticut. He blew up a Motel using two pressure cooker bombs! Before Courtney could say a work. Sarah asked her would she be willing to come to Connecticut? So, they can work together and come up with a plan to capture this lunatic! Courtney felt it was an honor to come and help.

Chapter 46

Sarah greets Courtney at the front door. Giving her a warm embrace. Sarah helps her carry the luggage into the house. Courtney took off her jacket. Sarah told her to make herself at home. Courtney wore her badge on her waist. She carried a .45 caliber hand gun inside a shoulder holster. She came prepared she was ready to take Randy down. She didn't know Sarah wanted to take Randy out with a bullet to the head. Sarah escorted Courtney to the bedroom on the first floor. She told Courtney it was identical to her bedroom upstairs minus the tub.

After Courtney put all her things away. Sarah gave her a tour of the rest of the house. Courtney thought the house was well decorated. They made their way to the kitchen, sitting at the counter across from one another. Sarah was filling in Courtney with the situation about the VA Hospital. And how the hospital was number one on his bucket list. She told Courtney they were going to the hospital tonight. Sarah gave her some more details about Randy Goldberg and how he could be detected. Telling Courtney, he has a malodorous odor that travels behind.

Courtney asks isn't he an amputee? Sarah said, "Yes! He lost his left leg out in the field, somewhere in Afghanistan." Hours had gone by; the ladies were on their way to the hospital. Sarah was driving while Courtney sat in the passenger seat looking at the tablet. She didn't know the drone had a multiple lens feature. She couldn't wait to get home and program her drone.

Sarah turns up the volume on the stereo – Don't Dream it's Over by Crowed House was playing. Sarah thought to herself... She hadn't heard this song in a while. Courtney was sipping on her Star Bucks coffee. She definitely needs it especially if she plans on doing an all-night shift with Sarah.

When they got close to the hospital, Courtney seen the large VA letters on the enormous building that rest on top of a hill. Sarah drove into the hospital parking lot. She told Courtney to wait a minute till her song went off – Sarah Smile by Hall and Oates. Courtney stays in her seat, taking sips of coffee. She noticed an officer walking a K-9 around the grounds. Sarah said, "that's a special bomb sniffing dog." They exit the vehicle, Sarah pointed in the air. Telling Courtney Casper was hovering above the hospital. Courtney was amazed at how Sarah had the hospital so secured. Sarah introduced Courtney to her security team. She addresses her professionally by saying F.B.I. agent Courtney Weatherly.

Courtney loved her introduction; she smoothly opens her jacket to reveal her badge. She got a kick out of showing her badge that way. Sarah took her on a tour of the hospital. They were in the staircase. When Courtney asked why she had so much security? Sarah just looks at her saying to herself... She still doesn't know how dangerous this man is.

Sarah begins telling Courtney, when she raided Randy's house. There was a list that was found. Randy thought he destroyed the list. When he set it on fire, the list didn't completely burn to a crisp. Sarah had the list decoded and Randy's last target was this VA Hospital. Randy was a veteran himself; he just felt the government never cared about the millions of people who fought in war for this country.

Especially, the soldiers who were wounded.... Mentally and physically. Randy was one of the wounded ones. He hated the so-called Wounded Warrior Project! He believed it was all a bunch of crap!!!

Courtney remembered Randy wrote something about the Wounded Warrior Project on the door inside the elderly couple home. Sarah told her Randy had a Psychotic behavior; he was supposed to be on several different medications. So, he could function in a proper manner. And it's been a while since he stopped taking his med's. So, Randy brain cells were completely twisted. He's too far gone to ever come back.

The more information Sarah shared with Courtney. It made her feel like she was in some kind of Michael Myers movie. But as long as, she had the .45 caliber hand gun. Courtney had no fear. They stroll through every floor; the patients and doctors were doing fine. Courtney had another coffee in her hand.

Sarah was talking with one of the police officers that was present at the motel explosion. Sarah gave him one of her cards, they shook hands. Sarah and Courtney went walking towards the cafeteria. Morning time came doctors begin changing shift as well as the staff. The hospital was once again moving at its' normal pace. Everybody entering or leaving the hospital had to walk pass the K-9 dogs. Casper didn't report nothing out of the ordinary.

Sarah and Courtney left the hospital. Courtney notices the lawn and how pretty the green grass was maintained. They got inside the vehicle; Sarah drove out the parking lot. She took Courtney to Star Bucks. So, she could get her morning fix. Sarah was on the highway heading home. Courtney was looking at the tablet. While taking sips of her coffee Sarah couldn't wait to take a nice hot shower and get herself some much-needed rest. Before they start there day trying to come up with a plan to catch Randy. Sarah drove into the garage. She opens the door and they went inside the house.

Chapter 47

Sarah was in her bedroom, she put her Glock .40 hand gun inside the closet. Which was always the first thing she did. She called it bedroom protection! Sarah took safety and security seriously. She got undress sliding open her dresser drawer. Grabbing herself some clean under-clothes and a towel. She stood in front of the dresser mirror. She noticed the changing of her face. She got closer to the mirror, looking at some dark rings around her eyes. Sarah knew the marks were there. Because of all the stress… she went into the bathroom. Hanging her garment across the glass shower door. She sat on the toilet and urinated.

Courtney was downstairs enjoying her Star Bucks coffee. She removed her holster with the .45 caliber hand gun resting inside. She places it on top of the night stand next to her badge. Courtney Star Bucks coffee had her energized! She begins unpacking her clothes, putting them into the drawers. She came across her taser underneath a pair of yoga pants. Courtney grabbed it out the suitcase. She put it on the night stand. She thought about the time, when she tasered her old boy-friend for putting his hands on her. 80,000 volts laid him out until the police arrived.

Sarah was inside the hot shower. The hot water had the bathroom full of steam. It gave her the feeling of being inside a sauna. Which was the next best thing to a full body massage.

The water was running down her body. Sarah grabs her hair shampoo squeezing it over her head. Then she places it back…. The shampoo had a nice ocean breeze scent.

Courtney had finally finished her coffee. She brought the empty Star Buck cup into the kitchen. Dropping the cup inside the trash can. She left out the kitchen stopping in front of the large bookshelf. Courtney was curious about what kind of books were in there. She seen a book called The Sleeping Beauty Killer by Mary Higgins Clark. Who is one of her favorite authors? She took the book with her into the bedroom. Courtney put the book on the bed. She went and crack open the bedroom window. She notices a funny smell coming from outside, but she didn't think much of it.

Sarah had turn around letting the shower water run down her back. She was thinking to herself saying she could stay in here all day. She begins twisting her hair rinsing it in the shower.

Courtney begins taking her clothes off. So, she could slip into something more comfortable. She knew once she starts reading the book. It was a strong possibility that she will fall asleep. She changed into some sweat pants and a white Polo t-shirt with the word Love written across the front. She bent down looking for her flip flops. Courtney knew she took them, out her luggage. She was feeling underneath the bed. When Courtney lifts her head up, she smelt the same foul odor. But only this time it was much stronger… Randy was standing behind her. He wrapped a cord around her neck.

Courtney first instinct was to reach for her hand gun. Until, the cord tightens around her throat! Forcing her to frantically reach for the cord. Courtney legs were kicking, while she dug her finger nails into the side of his face. Randy lean back, putting more pressure around her neck. He had her lift off the floor, Courtney stole one last breath…. She instantly went limp. Randy slowly placed her down on the floor. Courtney died with her eyes open.

Randy grabbed her holster, taking the chrome .45 caliber hand gun. He emptied all the bullets out the clip. Tossing the empty gun to the floor. Randy grabbed the taser, it made him think about the time, he was in basic training, when he was tasered with one of them. He began pressing the button. Looking at the electricity it possesses. Randy left out the room. He quietly walks up the stairs…. When he got close to Sarah's bedroom door. He could hear the shower running.

He opens her bedroom door, holding the taser in his left hand. Sarah was taking one last rinse. She was washing the suds out of her eyes. She turns the shower off, reaching for her towel. She stood inside the shower, while drying off. Sarah wrapped the towel around her body. She stepped out grabbing her panties. After she put them on…. She took a look at the mirror. Sarah seen the words – **Will you marry me.** It was written on the misty mirror. Sarah turns around in fear…. When she made it to the bathroom door? Randy greets her with the taser to her neck. She passes out falling to the floor.

Chapter 48

Hours gone by; Sarah closed eyes begin to twitch. As if she was fighting to open them. Sarah left eye open first then her right eye slowly open. Everything was really blurry.... She didn't know where she was at. It took her about another five minutes to get somewhat focused. Sarah felt a lot of pain in her neck area. A sharp throbbing pain, when she tries to turn her head. She was trying to avoid the thought of her neck being broke. Sarah closed her eyes and kept her head straight. She tried to move but couldn't.

Sarah opens her eyes and when she looks down at herself. She seen her wrist were duct tape in front of her. Sarah notice that she was wearing a white dress. When she looks down towards her legs. The white dress had a ball room gown look. Sarah was wearing a beautiful white wedding dress with a beaded neckline. When she looks at her hands, she stretched her fingers out. She notices a wedding ring was on her left-hand finger. Sarah tried to move her legs. She couldn't because they were duct tape together at her ankles.

Sarah finally realized that she was downstairs in her living room, sitting on her leather sectional. She couldn't scream or shout because her mouth was also duct tape. Sarah could only breath through her nose. Out of nowhere a foul aroma came creepin around her. The smell was so filthy it brought tears to her eyes. Sarah felt a hand rub across her shoulder. She wanted to turn her head to see who was there. But by the smell that was swirling around her. She knew it was Randy. She was too scared to let him see the fear that was written across her face.

Randy begins to massage her shoulders with his eyes closed. As if he was getting off, doing it. Randy finally walks from behind her. Sarah seen that he was wearing an old school black tuxedo with the tail in the back. She seen a wedding band on his left-hand finger. When she looks him in the face? He had four scratch marks across the right side of his face. Randy knelt down in front of her. He told Sarah that he loved her. She couldn't believe that she was looking a monster in his eyes. Randy breath smelt like road kill. He stood up still in front of her.

Randy told Alexa to play his music list. I cum blood by Cannibal Corpse begin playing. Sarah eyes open wide in shock! When she heard her amazon echo, actually playing his list. Sarah knew he must have been inside her house before.... what she didn't know was he been in there numerous nights. Randy grabbed the TV remote control. He sat next to Sarah. Turning on the television, it was on animal planet. He told Sarah this was his favorite channel. Which made Sarah think back... when one day she turns on the TV it was on animal planet.

Randy was watching a pack of hyenas eating the remains of a gazelle. After two male lions finished with it. Sarah cut her eyes at Randy who mouth was watery. While watching the Hyenas devour the dead animal. Onetime she caught him licking his lips. Randy looks at Sarah telling her that Hyenas were carnivorous mammals of Asia and Africa. Sarah got a closer look at Randy face. She knew the marks on his face was done with finger nails. Which let her know that Courtney fought for her life.

Chapter 49

Randy was sitting on the leather sectional with his arm around Sarah. She sat with him for what felt like hours, watching animal planet. Sarah knew she had to somehow get Randy to take the duct tape from around her mouth. After all Sarah years of studying Psycho-therapy. She knew what the duct tape around the mouth meant. Randy was the type who couldn't let anyone talk to him. Sarah knew she had to think of something fast. Before she ends up like Courtney. Randy strength came from his victims silence.

Sarah thought of an idea…. She knew actions speak louder than words. So, she made herself cry! Sarah eyes begin flowing with tears running profusely down her face. Sarah's weeping caught Randy attention. He took a quick glance at her. But he immediately turns back to the TV. He wouldn't miss watching the zebra, being eaten by a school of crocodiles for the world. Randy stared at the pool of blood in the river. He begins saying a crocodile is one of several thick-skinned long bodied carnivorous reptiles of tropical and subtropical waters. Randy turns his focus towards Sarah.

He spoke softly asking her what's the matter? Sarah was train not to give eye contact in these types of situations. Randy reach over to her mouth and pulled the duct tape off. Sarah stayed quiet… She wanted to follow his lead. Which was don't speak until spoken too. Sarah thought about the tone of his voice again. And how Randy had them dress in wedding out fits, wearing his victims from New Jersey wedding ring. She was about to take a gamble, by acting like his wife. Randy put his head down as if he did something wrong. Sarah said, "its ok I still love you!" Randy eased closer to her. He put his arm around her. Sarah asked could she hug her husband? Randy slid away from her and put his head down again.

This time he was twirling his wedding band around his finger. Sarah knew he was thinking, most mentally disturbed people go into a childlike state of mind. Randy finally stopped twirling his wedding band. He got on his knees in front of Sarah. She stood still without making eye contact with him.

Randy grabbed her legs. He begins to unravel the duct tape from around her ankles. When Randy finished, he sat back on the leather sectional. Sarah felt the blood circulating through her legs. She leant over telling Randy, she loves him. Following with a kiss on his cheek. Randy start rocking back and forth…. When he stopped, he told Alexa to play – I Don't Think I Love You by Hoobastank. Randy left the living room walking towards the kitchen. Sarah heard him moving around some dishes… He came back when the song went off. He sat beside Sarah and begin twirling his wedding band again. She watches him from the corner of her eyes. She knew he was thinking again.

This time when Randy stopped, he reaches over and begin untying her wrist. When Sarah hands were freed. She got a chance to see the wedding ring up close. She looks at Randy telling him, the ring is beautiful. Sarah held it in the air. Randy smiled and held his wedding band in the air too. Sarah was looking for the taser… She asked Randy for a hug? He opens his arms and Sarah went into them. She was trying to feel on him, searching for the taser. He took Sarah hand and lead her into the kitchen. Sarah seen a dead deer with a butcher knife stuck in its head. It was laying on top of her counter, with flies circling around it.

The dead deer look like it was found on the side of the road, dead for weeks. No one knew Randy treat road kill as if it was a delicacy. He sat Sarah in front of the carcass. She stared at the road kill. She knew there was no way, she was going to eat any of it. Randy put two plates on the counter. One plate in front of her. He then went and brought a candle to the counter.

Sarah just watches as he prepared his candle light dinner. Randy pulled the knife out of the deer head. Sarah watches him cut something from the carcass. He places it inside his mouth. Randy begins licking his fingers with a smile on his face. He went to go cut another piece. The knife dropped on the floor in between him and Sarah. She quickly reached for the knife and handed it back to him.

Randy proceeds to cutting the deer, he put a piece of something from the deer on her plate. Sarah was wondering what did he do with the taser and did he come inside her home with any other weapon? While she was unconscious, Randy went through the house. He emptied every gun clip in the house. Sarah stomach was about to turn... when she seen maggots moving away from the carcass on the counter. Sarah told Randy she needs to use the bathroom. She was hoping that he would bring her upstairs to use the bathroom.

Randy stuck the knife back into the carcass! He went inside the kitchen drawer and grabbed the black taser. He presses the button and Sarah seen the electricity. She couldn't believe that she was hit with it. Randy grabbed his wife hand and lead her upstairs.

Sarah was hoping and praying that he didn't find her .40 Glock hand gun. Sarah walks inside the bedroom. She told her husband that her feet were hurting from the shoes. Randy let her hand go, Sarah bent down. She took her shoes off, Sarah fake like she was getting up.... She did a leg sweep hitting Randy left leg. Causing him to fall backwards to the floor, dropping the taser Randy and Sarah was racing for the taser, he grabbed it.

Randy presses the button and swung down at Sarah. She quickly moved out the way. While Randy was getting off the floor. Sarah was crawling towards the closet. When she opens the closet door. She could here electricity coming in her direction. Sarah grabbed the .40 Glock hand gun turning around stopping Randy in his tracks. She said, **"Keep Your Vows Sacred. Sometimes Better Comes After Worse."** She squeezed the trigger. While Randy was lunging forward pointing the taser at her.

Sarah shot him twice in the head, causing Randy to drop the taser and fall to his death! Sarah got up off the floor. She kept her hand gun pointed at him. She seen the blood pouring from two holes in his head. Turning her cream-colored carpet maroon. She kicks the taser away from his dead body. Sarah went searching for her cell phone. She found it on the other side of her bed. She went running down the stairs, dialing 911!

Sarah went into the bedroom where she seen Courtney's lifeless body lying on the floor. She still had the cord around her neck. Sarah told the police dispatcher... There's been a murder and she need the police at 324 Troutman St. Sarah said, "a prayer for Courtney." Before she went on the front porch, waiting for the police too arrive. Sarah couldn't believe what she just went through... She gave the credit for her survival to the Quantic F.B.I training facility.

Moments later, four police cruisers drove into her driveway. A female officer came towards her. The three male officers went inside the house with guns drawn. While the female officer was getting information from Sarah. The three officers were securing the first floor, they came across the carcass on top of the kitchen counter. One of the officers asked what in the hell is that? Another officer said, "Road kill!" The three officers found a female body inside the bedroom.

Her cause of death, look like it appeared to be by strangulation.

The three officers slowly made their way up to the second floor. When they entered into the bedroom. There was a male body lying on the floor. His cause of death, look like it appeared to be by two-gun shots to the head. Sarah told the female officer, the female victim in the first-floor bedroom. She was a F.B.I. agent her name was Courtney Weatherly. And the male body on the second floor was the assailant… F.B.I.'s most wanted – Randy Goldberg.

The crime investigation went on for several hours. The coroner van arrived taking both bodies. Sarah left inside an ambulance. So, she could get evaluated.

Chapter 50

Four years later, Sarah was back in Quantico, Virginia. She was much older wearing prescription eye glasses. Sarah was back teaching her profiler class. The school had up-graded to giving each student a tablet. They no longer had to look at a projector screen. All Sarah rules were on the tablets. Sarah made it known what she expects from her students. She took her teachings very seriously. Because there were some Psychiatric human beings out there. Sarah added Randy Goldberg to her profile list.

He had become one of her worse cases ever. Randy was a very abnormal individual. Sarah wanted her students to know about his type. Sarah was waiting for her class to start. Once everyone was in the room and seated. Sarah introduced herself as Bomb Specialist F.B.I agent Sarah Richardson. Sarah never wastes any time. She told her students to turn on their tablets. Sarah always gave her class a quick quiz. So, she can find out what any of them know? Sarah told her students to touch the first photo.

A picture of Ted Kowinski appeared. She asks does anyone know who this is? Several hands went in the air... Sarah pointed to a white guy who had a navy haircut. He stood and said, "Ted Kowinski AKA the Unibomber." Sarah said, "You are correct." He smiled then sat back down. Sarah asked what did he do? The same several hands went in the air. Sarah pointed to a chubby white girl who squeezed out her desk. She said, "Mail bombs." Sarah said, "Correct."

Sarah told her students to touch photo number 6. A picture of Timothy McVoigh appeared. Sarah asks do anyone know who this is? Several hands went in the air. Sarah pointed to a black guy in the second row. He stood and said, "Timothy McVoigh." Sarah thought to herself saying this is too easy for them. Sarah told everyone to touch the very last photo. A picture of Randy Goldberg appeared. Sarah asked do anyone know who this is? One hand went in the air.

Sarah paused for a second... She pointed to the black girl in the last row. Who was Tammy the black girl from Walgreens? Tammy stood up with a smile on her face. She said, "Randy Goldberg." Sarah then asked her what did he do? Tammy said, "Suicide bomber... He used People; Places and things." Sarah said, "You are absolutely Correct!" When the class was over. Sarah walks over and she gave Tammy a warm embrace. She told Tammy, thank you!

Sarah never forgot all the important information Tammy accumulated. When she released her, Tammy told Sarah she always kept up with the newspaper articles. Then she congratulated her for taking down Randy! While they were on their way out the class room. Sarah told Tammy she's gonna be a great F.B.I. agent.

QUOTES

Acknowledgements

First, I would like to thank the Most-High. Because without him none of this would be possible. Secondly, I would like to give a shout-out to Mike Armfield, Kyle English, Keon GoForth, Warren Simpson, and Michael E. Stinson III for generously giving me your time and effort reading my material. You guys criticism meant a lot to me. Last but not least, I want to give a Special shout-out to Travis I Davis who was reading the story. While I was creating it chapter by chapter. Giving me great in-sight, feed-back and energy to complete this project. So, the world can get a vision of what's been ticking in my mind. When they read my Suspense/Thriller (Quotes).... I hope you enjoy reading my book. I would like to also thank my beautiful mother Mrs. Dorothy Haughton for typing my book.

About the Author

Tyrone Harvey was born and raised in New Haven, Connecticut. He is the father of four young adults. One son, three daughters and five grand kids who he loves with all his heart.

Mr. Harvey also have an urban fiction book published entitled Clean Money, Dirty mind (2006). He is versatile. Crossing over from urban novel to writing suspense/thrillers. He's always up for a good challenge with trying new things. He is a very gifted author who is hoping to one day entertain the world through his writing skills… He hopes you the readers enjoy his first suspense/thriller, QUOTES.

Printed in the United States
by Baker & Taylor Publisher Services